DARREL

ARCHER'S DYNASTY BOOK 6

KATHI S. BARTON

This is a work of fiction. Names, characters, places, and incidents are products of the author's imagination or are used fictitiously and are not to be construed as real. Any resemblance to actual events, locations, organizations, or persons, living or dead, is entirely coincidental.

World Castle Publishing, LLC
Pensacola, Florida
Copyright © 2024 Kathi S. Barton
Paperback ISBN: 9798891261327
eBook ISBN: 9798891261334
First Edition World Castle Publishing, LLC, January 10, 2024
http://www.worldcastlepublishing.com
Cover: Karen Fuller
Editor: Karen Fuller

Chapter 1

The wedding had been the most beautiful one that he'd ever been to. Marica, the newest Archer in the family, had been a lovely bride. And the way that she looked at his brother Sherman when they were walking around the reception area made him think that there couldn't have been a couple more in love than the two of them. It sort of made him jealous when he saw them.

However, Darrel didn't want the same thing for himself. Jealously was one thing. Having a wife and family wasn't for him. Not now, anyway. He had his life on hold for what he had wanted to be his entire life. To be a doctor. The best? No, just a good doctor for everyone who needed him.

Seeing the kids gathering around one of the play areas, he made his way there. Two days ago, his nephew Clay had taken a tumble down the front stairs to their home because of the ice, and he'd broken his arm. Going to check on him was simple for Darrel. He loved the little guy.

"What's happening here?" Clay held up his cast for him to see. "So everyone is signing off on it for you, huh? Good for you." He sat down when he was handed a marker. "When I was about twelve, I fell out of a tree and broke my arm. To be honest with you, I was more afraid of getting an x-ray than I was about hurting myself. I'd see those cartoons where something like that machine would light up your entire body and make you look dead."

"Grandma Katie said that was when you decided to be a doctor. On account of it not hurting you at all." He smiled at the memory and nodded at Clay. "She told us that you were really brave when you fell out of the tree, too. I cried when I fell. It hurt so bad."

"Because you fell down about five stairs on your arm before coming to a stop. Even then, with the ice all over the sidewalk, you hurt your knees and your face too, little buddy." He had taken a big tumble and it had scared him with the bruising on his little noddle. "Do you listen to your dad now when he says to you be careful of the ice?"

"Yeah, I sure do." After signing his name on the cast, he stood up to move around the large room. The reception was going to go on for another hour or so, and he was going to grab himself some food for his hotel room later. "Uncle Darrel, are you looking for yourself a pretty wife, too? I think all the women in our family is about the most beautiful in the world. Except for my little sisters. They're cute too."

"I don't know about finding me a wife, Clay. I work a great deal." And that was the very reason that he did work all the time. Avoiding finding himself a wife. "I'm hard to like anyway. A woman would be crazy to love someone like me. A doctor on call all the time and having such terrible hours."

"I don't think she'll care if you love her bunches." Smiling at the little man, he made his way to the bar to get himself a glass of ice-cold water. It was the best thing to drink in the world, he thought. When his phone went off, he stepped around the corner to answer it. He'd been contemplating leaving for the last hour or so. Smiling when he saw it was his mother, he asked her what she was doing.

"You're sneaking out the door is what you're doing, young man. Don't think that I don't have my eyes on you. Where will you go after this? Nowhere, that's where." He said that it was too stuffy in the place. "Be that as it may, you leave here, and I'll be disappointed in you. Aren't you happy for your brother?"

"Yes, of course I am. And I was really only going to go out into...where are you anyway? And why are you spying on me?" She said that she was going to the table with the grandchildren. "Signing his cast, I take it."

"Of course I am." When she poked him in the back, he closed up his phone and turned to look at his mom. "Are you trying to sneak out? I heard that you and William had an argument this morning. What was that all about?"

"Okay, first of all, it wasn't an argument. We were having a disagreement. There is a difference." She rolled her eyes at him. "All right. We argued. After I...he was right and I was wrong. I've not told him that yet, but I will. I'm touchy, all right. I told you what was going on at the hospital, and I'm worried."

"I don't know why you wouldn't be. I've been doing my own sort of digging, and I can't find anything about it either. Why would they shut down this hospital and not one of the smaller ones in Columbus? We need this hospital here. The next closest one is over an hour away if they do that." He agreed with her. "I know you do, honey. But it scares me to no end. I didn't know that they were even looking into it. To be honest, I had no idea that anyone could do that if it's a privately funded hospital."

He knew that his family mostly funded the local hospital. Also, patients paying too helped to keep the place running. But this thing that had come in the form of an email that said that as soon as January thirtieth, the hospital would be reviewed to see if it was needed. Needed? Of course, it was needed. It was a hospital, for heaven's sake.

And tracking down who the company was that had sent out the email had proven to be damned near impossible. Not even with their connections to the White House could they find anyone who could give them answers. Not to mention where this company was from.

He was just telling his mom that he'd contacted a friend from grad school to have them look into the company when his cell phone rang again. This was his friend, and he stepped out into the cold to tell him that he'd call him right back.

"I'm in town." Pausing from opening the door. "You told me that you'd be in DC today, so I came to town to talk to you and your family. When you told me that your brother was getting married, Darrel, you never said it was at *the* White House and that he was a Federal Judge marrying an FBI agent. I just thought you were a country bumpkin sort of doc that we'd hang out and tip cows or something. Then there is the fact that your family are 'the Archers.'" He told Carlin that he was just a family that happened to have connections. "Yeah, sure. And I'm a researcher for a Podunk company that looks into things. Christ, man. I don't have a gift or shit for the newly married couple."

"No one will care about that, I assure you. However, just to give you a heads up, the bride is the daughter of the Vice President, and the President is her godfather." He laughed when Carlin started cursing. "It's all fine. I swear to you. They only have eyes for each other, and if you freak out, which I have never known you to do, there are plenty of secret service around to knock you around a bit."

"I loath you." They were both laughing when he said that he'd meet him in front of the stairs. The man really was freaked out and it had done Darrel a world of good to have to calm him down. His mom went with him to the entrance of the venue. When they got to his buddy, they hugged, and then he introduced him to his mother. "I've heard a great deal about you, Mrs. Archer. Not as much as I should have been told, but I know who you are now."

"I'm just a mother of six boys, young man. Tell us what you have so that I can relay it to the others so they won't worry. We don't have to worry, do we?" Carlin told her that he'd be worried. But then he was a lowly researcher who really did work for a small firm. "I don't believe you're lowly anything. You found out things that I'm sure even the FBI couldn't if you found anything at all. Come on. We'll feed you, then get the scoop, as they say."

Darrel watched his brothers. They were all on what seemed to him high alert today. It had gotten so stressful since he'd gotten the email that Sherman wanted to cancel their big wedding and just wait around for things to be answered. He was glad that their mom had put her foot down on that one. He thought that his granddad was correct in saying that they needed this wedding to go on for a lot of other people.

While Darrel was walking along the long line of

food, getting himself some things for now and later, he thought of the things that had gone on in the past month while everyone was planning this wedding. It was a huge to-do, he thought, but it hadn't been big enough for people to ignore all the other things that were going on around it, like the death of Marcia's brother.

He'd been in and out of drug rehabilitation places since he'd been a teenager, a young one at that. Jules would go through the program, however long he would have to be there, and then come right out and go right back to taking drugs. The last time he'd come home with Marcia and Sherman to hang out for a few days. However, Marcia had caught him at it, and he'd killed himself.

They all, his family and that of Jules, had speculated that he'd come away from DC to end his life. Darrel thought that Jules knew what sort of light it would put his father in, the vice president of the United States, if he were found to have been a drug addict as a son, and that was his reasoning. Darrel had never said anything, but he thought that Jules was worn out. Going in and out of treatments like he had would have taken its toil on anyone. Finding a table, Darrel wasn't the least bit surprised when most of the rest of his family joined them at it. They all really were worried.

"Her name is Susan Snow." The picture of the young woman was passed around the table. "I will admit that I didn't look at this person very hard because all the evidence was pointing to her cousin Caitlyn. The deeper that I dug into Caitlyn's life, the more…it was just too easy for it to be Caitlyn."

"What do you mean? I mean…too easy?" He took the picture of Susan and looked at her. She looked like she was no more than ten years old, with her hair pulled into two neat braids and her ribbons hanging down. "If it was so easy, then that would mean that she's the one. That's what I think anyway."

"Yeah, that's what I think she wants you to think." Carlin handed a thick file to him. Opening it and then closing it just as quickly, he looked at his friend. "That's not either woman. I think that it was meant to be Susan, but whoever planted…I'm not telling you this very well. Let me start from the beginning. It will make more sense if I don't get to the end right away. All right?"

"You got this off the dark web." Marcia was an FBI agent, and he knew that if anyone would know what Carlin was doing, it would have been her. Carlin told her that he'd not started out on the web, but that was where he ended up at. "So you believe this woman is framing her...who are these two women. They have to be related, I'm thinking."

"Cousins. It was a simple thing to follow the IP or internet protocol address from the email that Darrel got when he handed over what he had. However, the more that I dug into that address, the more confused I became. I found out that it was a grocery store that everyone who worked there used for personal as well as work-related things. They even use the same address when a customer comes in and needs to have something faxed out. Then I found out that the internet ran to the apartment over the store that is being rented out. I figured that was where the computer was sending out the emails." Mom asked Carlin why he'd changed his mind. "The person that rents there, Caitlyn Snow, doesn't own a computer. Not a cell phone or cable. There's shit old pay phone that is on the outside of the building that she uses when she needs to. She told me Hell, I couldn't even find a television in the place that was being used."

"You went through her apartment?" Nodding, Carlin told Tally, William's wife, that she had invited him in. "Just like that, she said to come on in and look for a computer that I'm using to shut down a hospital? She is either really stupid or smart."

"She was selling something. Her brother's collection of trading cards, as a matter of fact. I didn't even...he died a few years back, she told me, and she was just getting around to selling his crap. Her words, not mine. I ended up being left there to look over the cards when she was asked to go down and run the register for the store for an hour. And while that sounds like she's trusting, it's far from it. The fucking big dog that she has up there with me wouldn't allow me to go beyond the four-square feet that I had been standing in. I used some of my equipment to figure out what I needed to know. If you ever meet up with this woman and she has her dog, I'd suggest that you stay back when she tells you to. He looks like he wouldn't harm a kitten, but I've seen him up close and personal. He'd kill for her, I believe."

"Okay, so she's protective of herself. And doesn't have a computer. I don't understand why you'd just say she's not involved with this going on." Another file was handed around. This one showed a very different picture than the one that he'd given him. No blood involved. "Who and how was that other person killed? I'm assuming that they're dead. They have at least ten bullet holes in their chest."

"I'm sorry. I got them out of order. Yes, that man is dead. He was dating who I thought he was Caitlyn until I found out differently." Carlin smiled at him. "I'm out of order again. Let me start again. I promise you it will be better."

Everyone agreed that they'd go to the hotel they'd been staying at and let Sherman and Marcia leave for their honeymoon. The two of them were going to go on a cruise and would be returning in a week. There would be nothing they could do to help them even if they didn't go, so it was decided that it would be fine if the two of them were to go. Mom would keep them informed if that became necessary. He hoped that it didn't, but of course, who the hell could tell anymore.

~*~

Carlin laid out all the information that he'd been able to gather up on the Snow cousins. He'd not been able to do this earlier and liked to have things in neat order before he went over things. It was his lack—or really his need to take too long to organize his things that had kept him from being promoted. Also, he thought that his bosses liked having him working for them as he could dig deeper into the dark part of the internet better than most. He really did enjoy that the most about his job. However, he'd never tell his bosses that. They'd move him someplace else, and he didn't want to do that.

The family began to show up just after he set up the projector. He'd been surprised and thrilled that the hotel had one on hand. This one was older than the one that he used at his place of business, but it worked, and he thought with a family this size looking things over, it might well do him good to have as much help like this as he could get.

"All right. We're ready, I guess." Carlin loved Mrs. Archer. She was a no-nonsense sort of person, and she never left you feeling like you didn't know her mind. She would tell you right off—"Before I forget, Carlin, friends of the family, Daniel, and Gilly will be joining us. You met them at the reception. The VP and President."

"Yes." He looked up when the door behind him opened. It was just the two men that Katie had been talking about. Nervous now, he sat down and stood up three times before Darrel came to sit with him. They were friends, and he hoped that if he did screw up too badly, he'd keep him from being murdered by the secret service. Smiling, Darrel told him to start. They were there for him. Nodding once, he looked at his list and started there. He knew there were going to be questions and hoped that it didn't mess him up too much when he had to go off his list and answer them.

"The path that I took led me straight to Caitlyn Snow. As I said before, it was just too simple. Too easy for me to understand why, if she was going to try and do something so underhanded as to close up a hospital, why she'd not take precautions in keeping her identity quiet. Also, the more I dug into her life, that of Caitlyn, the more I could see that she wasn't the type of person to do anything at all like this. Not that she wasn't smart enough; she is that and more. But it was the fact that she was very quiet and unassuming. Out of character for her completely."

He glanced at his notes and saw that he was to hand out the first set of papers about Caitlyn. Darrel took them from him and handed them out for him. He couldn't move on, not according to his notes, until they were all passed out. Carlin knew he was being strange, but he also knew that if he deviated too much from his list, he'd be lost again. He had to stay on track.

"Caitlyn and her brother, Andrew, were the only two children of Jim and Margie Snow. Jim's brother and his wife, Terry and Angie Snow, had two children as well. They're Susan and Terrance." He waited for someone to ask him to hurry things along, and when they didn't, he looked at Darrel. With his smile and nod, he decided that he was going to be all right. "Andrew was murdered four years ago by Susan. It was never proven, but because of her involvement, she was never welcomed again to any family functions. Even her parents had cut her off. Not long after Andrew was killed — it was ruled and accidental shooting by the courts — Jim died of a massive heart attack, leaving Margie alone."

"Was it the death of his son that caused him to die?" Darrel stood up after taking the paperwork out of the next stack that had to do with Jim's death. He answered his mom. "Oh. Such a shame to have died so young, too. I don't know what I'd do if one of you boys were to have been killed. How did he die, anyway?"

"Andrew and a bunch of his buddies were out cycling around the neighborhood. Andrew was sixteen at the time, it says here, and he'd only just gotten his permit the day before." Darrel looked at him, and he told him to go on. "According to the reports from neighbors around the time, Susan was *playfully* trying to run them down with her new car. Playfully? Seems to me if you're going to play running someone down on a bicycle with a car, that would be ruled homicide. How the hell did she — ah, here it is. She said that she'd messed up the break and gas pedal and had accidentally killed him. Still? I don't see this being anything but homicide."

"Her parents didn't agree with the courts either." Carlin sat back down and waited for the questions. He was all right with this way of telling them. Without Darrel's help, he'd be lost again. "Jim and his wife tried to sue Susan again, but his death occurred, and I don't know that Margie had it in her to keep going. She ended up in a nursing home not six months later. She is still there even as we speak."

"Is it because of Susan being thought of as guilty that you believe she's the one that is doing this to the hospital? I don't understand the connection. Or even if there is one." Heather, Peter's wife, looked around the table and then back at him. "Why go after a hospital? I mean, have you found the connection to her and it?"

"I remember this. You guys do, too. Andy, that's what he went by. His body had been—remember him, Del? You were about four years older than him if I remember correctly. I think that he'd been pronounced dead at the scene, so by the time he was brought here, he was already gone." Del said that he could barely remember it and asked if he was the one that the body had come up missing. "Yes. About an hour after he was brought here, he'd been taken to the basement. His body and all his clothing had come up missing. There was a single shoe left behind."

"Yes, that's it." Carlin was glad for Darrel's help in this. "His parents only had the shoe in which to bury him. Neither the body nor any of the paperwork that had come in with him was ever found. The gurney too that he'd been laying on down there had bleach poured all over it, they discovered when they went to find him."

"They've never found his body then? My goodness, no wonder Jim died. That would...so Susan can't be tried properly because there is no body and thus no evidence. What did the ambulance drivers say about his body coming up missing?" Carlin told Merce what he'd found out. "Good for them in keeping their records for bringing him here.

The doctor that signed off on receiving his body, whatever happened to him?"

"He's dead. Not long…this is getting more convoluted the more we hear about this. So, the hospital's connection to the family is that their son/nephew had been killed and brought here. Then, in what could only be called something very strange, he comes up missing. Before or after the autopsy?" Carlin told Katie that it was before. "So there is nothing to prove that he was brought to the hospital except from the ambulance services, that he was killed, nor what he might have been killed by in the accident. And this Susan person is the one that you believe is behind the — does she want the hospital closed down because she thinks the body is still there? That she's afraid that someone will find it or something?"

"That I don't know." Katie told him that he'd done a great job for them on this. "Thank you, ma'am. I do appreciate you saying that. But there is more about Caitlyn. She's been working hard in trying to get her brother's death overturned, and her cousin blamed for it where it belongs. Currently, she's working three jobs to be able to pay someone to go into the hospital to have a thorough search. She's never believed that his body wasn't just there where it was brought in."

"We'll help her." Carlin told Merce that it wasn't as easy as that. "What do you mean? We just help her hit her goal, and then we get that woman put behind bars where she belongs. She won't turn down a little help from us, will she?"

"I don't know for sure, but I think that she will. She's been approached before about getting help. From her uncle and his wife, believe it or not. Getting her law degree at present is what she's been working for since this all came about. Caitlyn has no trust in anyone other than herself." Katie said that she could understand that as well. "Yes, I knew that you would. I've spoken to her, as I said. She didn't say much as to why she was selling his things after all this time. I couldn't find anything about her other than she's been taking care of her mother's bills since she's been confined to the nursing home. She doesn't visit her. I don't know why, but she does keep up with her bills as well as any extras that she might need. Like her hair done, a new toothbrush, or anything personal like that."

"Do you have any suggestions as to how we get in touch with her?" He told Robert that she had a list of things that she was still selling. "What sort of things are there? The reason that I ask it is, do you think that it would do any of us any good to go and see what we can help her with if it's something that we want?"

"There is a house that belongs to her. I don't have it on the list. There are also some of his things that would be considered collector items if you know what you're looking at. I will admit that I purchased the trading cards from her. They were in mint condition and — well, you don't care about that. Some of the things on the list are outdated, but she's not asking all that much for it. A computer. Let me think. Video games for the system that is also in great shape. They might not have had much, but they took care of the things that they had." Katie asked about the house. "It's been in the family for a few generations, but it really needs an overhaul she told me. And because of that, she's not asking all that much for it. The listing for it is in one of the files here that I can find for you."

"You're holding back on something." He looked at Peter and he asked him what he meant. "I don't know. I can almost taste your hesitance in telling us something. We need to know all that we can about this business. What is it that you're thinking?"

"Well…This isn't something that I would recommend to anyone who didn't have the funds to do it, but I'd hire someone to go in and find the body. If it's there. You have to admit, even after this short amount of time, we have advanced in equipment that can do a search well beyond even four years ago." He glanced at Del and his wife, Merce. "I know that this is out of your realm of things that the two of you come up with to help out in the hospital, but perhaps you know someone that can, I don't know, do you a favor and figure this out before she can turn your help away."

Carlin sat down when the family started putting their heads together to get an idea of what would be needed to search a place as large as the hospital to find a body. As he said, if it was still there. He handed Darrel a list of things that had been done to the hospital over the last four years and told him what it was.

"This will be a good place to start looking. You think that he's in one of the construction sights that was going on when he died." Carlin told him that it only made sense that it had to be going on when it happened because whoever hid the body wouldn't be able to dig out a wall or whatever without people noticing. "You're right. We'll start with them. Christ, Carlin, you did us a great service for this. I can't thank you enough."

"You can thank me by finding him. And what happened to him that would have someone hide away his body for all this time." He said that he'd do that. "That's all I need. That poor family has been through enough for several lifetimes, and this needs to be put to rest."

"I agree." Darrel was the only person in his world that he could talk freely with. Darrel knew that he had social anxiety and didn't understand social ques from other people. Even in high school, Darrel had been there for him, and he would give him the world if he asked for it. "You'll hang around for a few days, won't you? I miss talking to you."

"I have to go back to work." Darrel nodded and told him that he'd call him sometime. "You do that. I would love to hear from you."

Carlin made his way home after they all had dinner together. He knew that Darrel would call often, but Carlin knew that he'd have to see his doctor again for this little time he'd been out of his comfort zone. He'd helped him if he asked, but he wasn't one to do anything out of his zone. He thought that

Darrel knew that as well.

Chapter 2

Darrel found himself looking at every wall in the hospital as he did his rounds of late. It was futile. He knew that. He couldn't see through walls. He'd not know a new wall from an old one. But he just couldn't help himself. Three days ago a crew had shown up at the hospital to see if the wall structure of the hospital was up to par. At least, that was what they were telling people when they asked. While he had an idea what that meant, he didn't have any idea how they were going about it. They just seemed to be taking a lot of pictures of walls and floors to him.

"Doctor Archer, there's a phone call for you. She might have told me her name, but I can't for the life of me understand her because she's that angry." He asked if he could transfer it to the doctor's lounge. "Yes. I was going to suggest that. If she's going to hand you your ass, then you should do it in private."

After getting to the lounge, he picked up the phone and heard the woman on the other end gripping about being put on hold for the forth time and that it was fucking cold. Smiling, he said his name and asked if he could help her.

"Yes, you can fucking well help me. I'm trying to get in touch with your mother. At least, that's who I think I'm trying to get to talk to. She just keeps hanging up on me. I want to know what the hell is going on there." He asked her who she was and where she was talking about. "Caitlyn Snow. And the hospital you're at."

"Okay. I can understand my mom hanging up on you if you're this polite when you've spoken to her. As for what is going on at the hospital, I don't know how to answer that either. We have lots of things going on right now with patients and the such. Are you inquiring about one of them? I'm afraid that—" She growled. Darrel couldn't help it. He laughed. "You're going to have to be more specific if you want answers from me."

"There is a crew going around taking pictures of walls. Why are they doing that?" He told her. "That's bullshit. They don't just do that. Believe me when I tell you I tried to get that done years ago."

"Is this about your brother?" He didn't mean to ask her that, but since it was out there, he continued. "Let me explain to you why I ask that. I got an email a couple of weeks ago that the hospital was going to be shut down for lack of necessity. I myself can't figure out why anyone would think that not having as many hospitals as a good thing. But after having someone look into things, that might be a reason for them to think that it came up about you, your cousin, and your brother. After doing some more digging, we figured that we'd help you along with getting justice for him by pulling a few strings and having our own search going on. It was pointed out that if we close our doors for whatever reason, someone might well come in and tear the place down."

"I don't understand." He said that he didn't either, but that's what they'd been able to find out. "You're saying that you've connected some kind of dots to your hospital shutting down back to my brother's missing body. How the hell...you know what? I don't care. The least you could have done was contact me about what your plans were."

"It was pointed out to us that you'd not accept our help and that we might well be better off just doing what we could and hope that you'd come on board with us. Also, we have someone looking into your cousin's involvement, too." She told him that she was not her cousin. "If you've disowned her, I can understand that. If you would allow it, I'll pick you up and take you to my mom's house. From there, we can all have a nice dinner and talk about what we've come up against in all this. Share information that might benefit both parties."

"Susan won't like this." Darrel said he wasn't afraid of Susan. "You should be. She's a fucking vindictive cunt that won't stop at just you telling her that she needs to back off. She's made my life a living hell since Drew was killed, and my family blamed her for his death."

"Do you know what happened that day? There are a great many different versions to the story." She said that she wasn't there, but she had the police report. "So do we, but it's not all that helpful without a body. By the way, you didn't seem all that surprised when I said we thought it was her shutting down the hospital."

"Nothing about her surprises me. And if you've found out anything about her, it shouldn't you either." He heard her talking to someone about using the phone. "I'm freezing here and need to go inside. If you want me at your house, I don't drive so if you'll pick me up around six then I'll tell you what I know. I'm not staying there even if the snow that is supposed to come in does. I'll walk home rather than be where I'm not at home. Get it?"

"All right. I can make sure you get home safely. However, one thing that you should understand, Ms. Snow, is that this is our investigation, not yours, and we make the rules. You don't." He set the phone back in the cradle and sat there for several minutes, thinking about their conversation. Darrel came to two decisions right then.

First of all, he wasn't going to be having dinner with his family. He didn't want to be in close proximity to the woman. And secondly, he was going to avoid her as much as he could. This was how it began; he knew. An innocent meeting with a woman, even if she pissed you off, then poof, you were all over each other and getting married. He didn't want that at all.

Making arrangements with his mom to have Caitlyn picked up, he realized that he not only didn't have a phone number to reach her with but also didn't have much in the way of information on where to pick her up. Mom said she'd take care of it, and he hung up before Mom could tell him that he'd better be there. It was going to be a long night until someone contacted him about what the plans were. But he'd rather be alone than with a strange woman who may or may not be his wife soon.

Wandering down to where the men were working on the walls, he was just settling into being bored when one of the people found something. He continued to watch from afar, hoping that this would end the search and things could progress to the point where he didn't have to worry all the time.

"Hey, Doc? Can you tell us what this might be? It's not human, I don't think." He looked at the image that they'd captured and told them it was a cat. "Christ. Poor thing. It probably got itself down in that cubby hole, and the concrete was poured over it while it was sleeping. Terrible death for the thing."

"What do you do with that information?" He was told that they'd have to mark the wall and tell what was there. It wasn't their decision to remove anything from the walls but only to have a look around at the workmanship. "I would imagine that you run into this sort of thing a lot when having to go back over work."

"Usually, we'll find a rat or two, but nothing

more. This is only the second feline I've ever seen."
He set up the equipment to go to the next wall. "We
have found several bodies that have been sealed up
in walls. The police get called in, and they hire a crew
to go in and sort the mess out."

"Do you know what it is you're looking for
here?" The man just nodded without saying a word.
"Good. I would hate for you to see something that
you're not prepared for. I would image that you're
not really surprised by anything that you find in
walls. But I am."

"Do you happen to know where things were
being worked on when this happened?" He told
him that according to the plans he'd been given,
they had been adding a wall of cadaver drawers.
"Do you know which wall? We can start there if that
might get things cleared up sooner. I know that the
government is picking up the tab on this one, using
this as a training program for the younger searchers,
but we don't have to spend that much time here
looking if you have an idea."

Darrel pointed out the wall of drawers that
he knew of. They had discovered about four years
ago, about the time of the accident, that they weren't
compliant with having enough room for storage. So,

in an effort not to be fined more money, they had hired a crew to come in and expand. As it turned out, they rarely used the new set, but he supposed it was nice to have the extra room.

Once the equipment was set up, they were taking their third set of pictures of the area when his cell phone rang. Answering it without looking at who was calling, Darrel simply said his last name. It took him a few seconds to realize that the person on the other end of the line hadn't said anything.

"Hello? Who is this?" Still nothing. Deciding to hang up, he decided that if they wanted to talk to him, then they fucking should be ready when he answered. Closing the connection, he heard it again immediately, and he saw that it was Gilly. He asked him where he was. "At the hospital. I'm on call tonight, and I'm just hanging out here. Why? What's happened?"

"Nothing happened. But I'm glad that you're hanging out. I'm assuming with the workers." He said that he was and that they'd already found a cat in the walls. "Oh my. Well, at least we know that they can find things. I have a favor to ask of—"

"Doc? We found something." Telling Gilly what was going on, he said to call him back later.

Making his way to the computer that would, if needed, print a picture of what they were getting, he waited with the rest of them as the printer spit out its paper. It wasn't nearly finished with the image when one of the men spoke again. "That's a skull if I don't miss my bet."

~*~

Caitlyn didn't move from the spot she'd been asked to stand on. There were just too many people in the room for her to move anyway. But this way, she figured that someone would find her if they needed her. So far, the only person that she'd spoken to was Merce, and that was just because she'd been asked where Darrel was.

"He said that he had to make a couple of calls and that he'd return." Merce nodded, then drifted away. Under her breath, Caitlyn had thanked herself and then felt stupid because she'd been passive-aggressive to the other woman. "Sorry."

She'd only just shown up at the Archer home, Peter picking her up and taking her there, when Darrel called and told them that they'd found a skull. While there was no other information given at the time, they all bundled up and drove the short distance to the hospital where her brother had been last seen.

"Hello." She glanced at the man who had shown up about ten minutes after the Feds had come in. "You're Caitlyn Snow, if I remember correctly. My name is Gilly Jamieson. I'm so sorry about the loss of your brother."

"Do they think that it's him that they've found?" He told her that, for now, they were trying to see how the body was lying so that they could dig around him to pull him free of the concrete. "If it's my brother, what happens? I mean, will they be able to do an autopsy after all this time?"

"From what I understand, yes, they'll be able to. However, it will be done somewhere else and not here. They'll want to make sure that all the t's are crossed and i's dotted on this one." She nodded. "I can make sure that you're informed at every step if you wish. I know this must be a very difficult time for you, so I'd like to make that easier on you if I can."

"Thank you. I just wanted him found. And now that he might well be, I'm terrified of what this might mean for my family. My dad passed not long after he was killed. My mom is in a nursing home because of this. I just hope that now that he's found, everything, including who and why someone would do this, is made to pay." He asked her if she meant her cousin. "If she did this to us, then that's right. I want her to pay."

She looked at the man then, and it occurred to her that she should know who he was. But there were other pressing issues running through her mind, and she didn't have it in her to try to remember who he might be. At his laughter, one that she'd only heard on television in the diner.

"You're sneaky, aren't you?" He nodded and told her that he had to be a part of this as his daughter was married to one of the Archers. "Yeah, the big wedding everyone was talking about. Congratulations on that, by the way. I only just met the Archers today. They're very pushy, aren't they?"

"They are, but they do get things done. Like this." She said that she'd been working on getting this done for years. "Sometimes it only takes a little push in the other direction to get things moving. This affected one of theirs, Darrel, the doctor, and they rounded up the wagons and found a way to make it so that he was safe and doing what he loved. Same as with the young woman married to Robert. His wife is a doctor here as well."

She watched the men as they stood over the drawer that had been taken apart when the skull was discovered. Caitlyn wanted them to just dig him out, even if it wasn't her brother, so that they could have some peace. But they had to ensure that evidence wasn't tampered with and that if they wanted to be able to take whoever done this to court, it had to be done so that nothing was done wrong. It would be terrible to have her brother brought out and not ever be able to persecute whoever did this to him.

"Your family, uncle and aunt, will you tell them when they find out who this is?" Caitlyn asked Gilly what she was asked to call him if he thought it was her brother. "I do. I believe you do as well. I can't imagine there being two missing bodies in the same place, can you?"

"No." She watched the crew closely, trying her best to see if she could see anything that would tell her that— "All this time, I've been telling myself that he's out there someplace. Alive and well. That once he got here, he woke up and wandered off someplace, not knowing who he was or where he was from. I never saw him after he was killed. I didn't have any way of telling my heart and mind that he was gone forever. I needed to believe that he walked away.

Understand?"

"Yes. I lost my son recently, too." She told him how sorry she was about that. "Thank you, dear, I am as well. Jules reminded me so much of my late wife, too much at times. But I loved him with all my heart. I tried so hard to tell myself that he was going to get better. That he was going to stop taking drugs and that crap so that he'd be well. But I also knew, deep into my heart, that he wasn't going to do anything like that. It was too much a part of his life, I guess."

"I understand that, too." When they started digging again, this time with small equipment that Merce and her team were able to provide, they were asked to wear masks. But Gilly told one of the Archer men that she and he were going to go and get something to drink. The elder Archer, Delmar, said that he'd join them. There wasn't anything he could do standing around.

In all, Katie came with them, as did Merce. They were just sitting down at one of the tables after getting herself a sandwich and glass of soda when she heard Darrel's name being paged over the intercom system.

"He's on call today. I think he told me that he has about two hours to go." Caitlyn didn't know why they thought she'd care but thanked Katie for the information. "I have some information for you about your…well, Susan, if you'd like to have it. I've been speaking to a couple of people who are aware of her, and she's doing quite well for herself."

"She's always been one to land on her feet. Right after Drew came up missing, she went on a long vacation that took her to several countries." Merce asked her if she'd traveled much. "No. Never. I've been saving up every penny I can so that I could afford to rent one of those machines you guys are using. At the rate I was going, it more than likely would have been another fifty years or so to afford it."

"I'm to understand that you're selling off your parent's home, too." Caitlyn didn't even bother asking her how she knew that. But she told her anyway. "Word gets around about such things. Actually, the private investigator is the one who told us about your list. Carlin is a good friend of Darrel's. They went to school together. Why are you renting a place when you have a house to live in? Or are there just too many memories attached to the house? I can understand that, too."

"After my father died and Drew being gone,

mom and I roamed around the house like a couple of zombies. Then she started to get ill herself. They said it was late-stage dementia by the time they got around to diagnosing her with it. I didn't realize it; my dad usually took care of mom when she was upset. It sent her over the edge, I guess you'd call it, when they were no longer close to her. I had moved out of the house only about a year before all it came crashing down on her." Katie asked about the nursing home. "Dad had it set up that if he were to die before her, a policy would make sure that Mom was given over to the care of some place and paid for by it. I make sure that she has whatever she needs, but I can't go see her. When she sees me, it puts her in such distress that they have to sedate her for several days afterward. It hurts me to no end, but she's happy otherwise."

"What a wonderful daughter you are." Caitlyn finished her sandwich and played around with her straw. "What will you do if this is your brother, Caitlyn? You must have given it some thought."

"I didn't think beyond finding him. Of course, he'll need to be buried. But beyond that, finding his killer is all I can think about right this minute." Katie's cell phone went off, and Caitlyn tensed up. After she hung up, she stared at her. "It's him, isn't it? They found him."

"They can't be certain, but it does look like it's him." Caitlyn didn't move when the rest of them stood up. "What do you want to do, honey?"

"She and I will have us a slice of pie, and then we'll mosey our way up there. You go on ahead, child, and I'll see to Caitlyn." She was never so grateful for someone speaking up for her as she was at that moment. Delmar said they'd be fine. After they left, he patted her on the back and spoke softly to her. "You're going to be just fine, child. I promise you. We'll be right here for you when you need us."

"I don't know what to think." He said that was understandable, as it was a blow to her heart. "Yes. I wanted it not to be him but to be him, too. Like to get some closure on this. All I can think about now is that he really is gone, and I have to move on from here."

"You let me call your aunt and uncle for you. I know them both. You are going to tell them, aren't you?" She said that was the plan. "I'll do that for you. You and me, we'll go over and see them right now if you want."

"I'd like that. However, I can do it. I don't want to put you out, Delmar. They're my relatives, and they need to know that I don't know that maybe this is the end of things." He asked her if she thought that would be the end. "No. But that's all they've lived for is to find their nephew. They have it in their head that Susan killed him. I haven't any idea, not after all this time, if they think that she had anything to do with his disappearance. I do. On both accounts."

"You and me, we'll head over there now. It would be terrible if they heard from someone else that they've found him. Then, when we get back, you and me will head on down to see what's what with the body. As I heard said to you, there can't be that many bodies that have been hidden away in the walls of this old hospital." She agreed with him, and they headed out a few minutes later.

Pulling up in front of the house that she'd grown up near hurt her heart. She'd not had a great deal of contact with her aunt and uncle, but she would see them often enough that they had an idea of where things stood with finding Drew. As soon as the big limo, the only vehicle that Delmar was allowed to have now that he had given up his licenses, she was out of the car first. Her uncle, coming out onto the front porch, dropped to his knees the moment he saw her.

"You found him." She hugged him as he sat down on the cold stoop. "Oh lord, you've found him. That's it, isn't it, Caddy-did. You found your brother."

"He was buried in the walls of the morgue. They're digging him out now, but it looks to be him. I was told that the injuries on the body, which is all they can see through the x-rays, are consistent with it being him." Uncle Terry hugged her tightly, and she and Delmar got him to stand up to go into the house. "They're going to have to do an autopsy on him. I don't know any more than that right now."

When her aunt joined them a few minutes later, she had to go and find her medication so that she could calm her nerves. Delmar answered questions for them, even going so far as to call Darrel for answers that he didn't have. One of them she was surprised by.

"That's a good question, there, Terry. Darrel said that his body would be well preserved as it has been encased in the concrete for so long. And with the cooling unit in the room, it has made things stay in good shape. That it will be easy enough to do tests on him as well. Something else that he said pin points this as being your boy is that they found a single shoe in the body bag through the x-rays." Getting up and leaving them all sitting in the living room, Caitlyn made her way to the kitchen.

She knew that she'd be able to find what she wanted and dug around in the cabinets until she was able to find herself something for her sudden headache. There was nothing that she'd ever be able to find that would heal her heart for her. Her little brother had been killed. Then, in an act that could only be described as an act of a monster, he was hidden away from them for all these years while his killer had remained free.

"Are you all right?" She looked up at the man standing there and didn't think she knew him. "Darrel Archer. I came by to see if your family was all right. I didn't know that granddad had come with you."

"He's been answering questions for them. If I knew the answers, I didn't remember them. Are you pissed off because he came with me?" He shook his head and then sat down. "I'm sorry. That was uncalled for. I've been on edge with people for a long time, and I don't know how to act around them anymore. It's why I work from home for my primary job and do classes on line."

"They said you were going to be an attorney." She again wasn't surprised to find out that he knew that about her. "As I told you before, we had to connect the dots to where you stood in this closing of the hospital."

"I get it. I don't like it, but I get it." She struggled with the bottle some more and then finally put it on the table. "If my cousin was here, he'd make fun of me for not having the strength to open a bottle. Terrance and I got along great. That's Susan's brother if you didn't know." Darrel took the bottle and asked her how many she needed.

"I'd like to tell you to only take one, but I don't want to piss you off again by telling you what to do." She took one. "Good girl. I have something stronger if you think your aunt could use it. She isn't doing well, I don't think."

"She's a bit of a drama queen. If you offer it to her, even if she doesn't need it, she'll take it so she can tell people later that she had to be sedated. One example I'll tell you about that will make you know what I'm talking about. When we had the funeral for my brother, we only had the shoe. Aunt Abby wanted it so that she could carry it around. Mom relented because it was easier with her to do so. Aunt Abby walked around the funeral home, wailing about how that was all they had left of her dear precious nephew. I'd not offer." He said that he wouldn't. "Thanks. I love her to pieces, but she can suck most good moods out of someone in a flash if she feels she'd not getting enough attention about something going on."

"Sounds like someone I went to school with. Nothing got past her that she didn't have some sort of connection that she could play on." After getting herself a drink, she offered Darrel one. "Thank you, I'd like that."

She fixed them both a glass of ice water. He said that was all he drank, and she sat at the table with him. They didn't really talk about anything but the weather and where she was in her studies. When her Aunt joined them in the kitchen, Cailyn glanced at Darrel when her aunt started saying how stressed she was about all this.

"You should have a small glass of wine, Aunt Abby. It always calms your nerves." She tisked at her. "Or not. Now that I've told you everything that I know, I'm going head back home until I hear from someone about what is going on."

She stood up, and so did Darrel. "I was going

to suggest that you go back to the hospital with me. The men there are wanting a few questions answered, and since you're his blood relative, it would fall on you to answer them." Aunt Abby said that she'd go too. "That's not necessary, ma'am. You won't be able to see him until the police are finished with him. And to have him identified that would fall on his sister."

"But what if she can't tell? You'll need me there to make sure she's not grief-stricken too." Caitlyn told her that she would be just fine. "Oh, Caitlyn, you don't know how it's going to affect you after it has been so long. Just let your uncle and I go with you, and you'll see that — do you think that the news people will be there?"

"No, they won't be. The Feds are keeping everyone away." She was grateful for Darrel in that moment for talking to her aunt like he was. Stern but polite. He seemed a pro at handling women like her aunt. Nosy and wanted to be the center of it all. "Are you ready?"

They left not long after that. Delmar and her uncle hugged, and he offered to be there if they needed any more information. He also told them not to talk to the press. That they'd mess up their words, and it would be terrible for them all.

"They usually do anyway." Uncle Terry looked at her before speaking again. "I need to call Terrance, honey. He'll want to know from us before someone else tells him. Is that all right?"

"Yes, that'll be fine. But make sure that you tell him that they're doing tests and that while it's assumed to be him, about ninety-nine percent sure, they still need him to be identified as well as bloodwork done." Aunt Abby said they didn't want her going. Delmar agreed. "The less we can have people around, the easier it will be to keep it under wraps. Yes, you not going there too will make things easier on the police to make sure that any and all evidence is preserved."

"Are you all right?" That was the second time that Darrel had asked her that, and she didn't have an answer this time either. "The reason that I ask is that you've been handling this well so far. I don't know you well enough to know if this is normal for you or not. I don't want to have you break down and hurt yourself."

"I don't know how I feel." He nodded and told her that he was there if she decided that she needed something. "Thank you. I'll be all right. Now that his body, if it is him, will be put to rest, and we'll get to have justice for him. I hope."

"You will." She nodded, not sure why he'd care, but it was nice to have someone encouraging her in this. When his cell phone rang, she tuned him out. Delmar was there, too, but he was watching his grandson. Caitlyn had nearly missed that they were back at the hospital. She'd been so deep in her thoughts about the times Drew had been around. She missed him so much.

Chapter 3

Susan stood in line for her daily helping of slop. While hating to be in a homeless shelter in the first place, having a blanket and a roof over her head was more than she had on her own right now. Also, she didn't complain too much. They'd kick her out again if she did that, so she smiled at the woman who asked her if she wanted meat or not. Why they thought it was meat was well beyond her. It looked like a wadded-up roll of toilet paper covered in brown goop.

Sitting at one of the tables, she reached for the catsup bottle to drown all the food in it. Susan also knew better than to put up a fuss about the bottle being dirty and nearly empty. There were peas, too, that she hated but would eat with enough of the red sauce over it to make it look less like frog balls and more like cut-off balls. Her brother used to call them balls when he was little. That both hurt her and caused her to smile.

Her life sucked right now. Well, it had since she'd been in her accident. Susan never referred to is as murder—not even in her mind. Nor did she even think to herself about how she'd hit her cousin that day. She only thought of it as an accident. A fun one but one that had caused her to have a shit load of stuff she hadn't anticipated raining down on her head. Her parent kicking her out was only one of her serious issues right now.

Taking a few bites of the meat, she thought about her family. Susan hadn't seen her parents in two years. And even that had been from afar. Not that she missed their rules and such, but she did miss the money. They'd taken out a restraining order against her so that she couldn't be within fifty feet of them the day after the trial had been over. She so missed living at her big fancy home with servants and shit all the time. There were times, too, when she missed talking to her family. Especially Terrance. But they never believed her, so she supposed she was better off without them in her life. Not that she wasn't guilty as fuck, but still…she was their family, after all.

Though a little bit of money wouldn't go

without notice, she thought. Holding down a job, even trying to apply for one, would bring up the accident, and they'd tell her that they didn't want her to be around the public. Or that they had a reputation to adhere to, and she wasn't a fit. She hadn't tried all that hard either in finding a job. It was just too much fun for her to steal what she wanted. But even that was getting more and more difficult.

As it often did, thoughts about her cousin Caitlyn would enter her mind when she thought of being penniless and homeless. Comparing her life to her cousins — Susan was in a homeless shelter sharing a room with ten other people all lined up like logs on the worst kind of mattress.

She was sure that her wonderful, never does anything wrong cousin was sitting pretty in her parents' home having servants wait on her hand and foot. She wished that she could have ten minutes with her just to show her what it felt like to be thought of as a murderer.

Pushing her tray away when she couldn't stomach any more of the slop, Susan did something that she'd not done since that day. She thought of the day that Drew had come up and over her car when she'd run him down. The little pisser had not just died, but he'd ruined her life by not doing what she wanted of him. Everyone had learned that lesson, that she was right and got what she wanted a good deal quicker than Drew did. Now, he was dead. Through no fault of her own, too.

It had been just long enough that she could no longer remember what she'd wanted from Drew that day. But he'd told her no, and she didn't like that. No amount of threats either had made him change his mind, and that pissed her off more. So she followed him home after his friends had left to go home too.

Susan knew that she had killed him. She knew as soon as she rammed her car into the back wheel on his bike that she might have taken things a little too far. And when he went flying up and over her car, it pissed her off again that he'd not fallen over in front of her so that she could 'accidentally' run over him. It had taken her backing up and over him twice before she felt like he'd paid for what her car had looked like as well.

Taking off, leaving his body where it had fallen, she made her way to the hospital. In her mind, it made sense that she be there to make sure that he was dead and not able to tell on her. At the accident, she had seen that his chest was as flat as a pancake and that his legs were crushed into the pavement; however, she needed to do as much damage control as she could. She knew that he was dead and wouldn't be able to say what happened to him. However, Susan knew on some level that he'd be able to *tell* a lot if they were to really look at his body and the damage she'd done to it.

The idea of hiding his body was one that she made as soon as she entered the morgue. Susan didn't know if she had seen it on one of those crime shows that her mother watched about no body, no trial, but that was where her mind went.

Not knowing how long she'd had to wait for him to show up to take care of him, but when he did, she was going to be ready. About an hour or two later, Susan watched as the man who had signed for Drew's body had left, and Drew's body was there for the taking. Since she didn't know how long she had, Susan made herself take deep breaths so that she'd not fuck this up. To this day, she wondered why no one ever thought to look in the construction areas going around in the morgue, but it was a good thing for her that they had, she supposed.

Rolling the cart over to the construction area, she rolled Drew off the bed, body bag, and all into a deep place in the wall. She was going to take him out of the bag, but the sight of his head and body sickened her. It was then, she supposed, that his shoe had fallen out of the bag. That had scared her to death when she'd heard that all they'd found was a single shoe of his and nothing else.

After making sure that the bag wasn't noticeable, she put all the paperwork that she could find around in with him. She had done a little dance around the room when she finished up before being caught. Who would have figured that she could be so devious about shit and get away with murder?

Leaving the same way that she arrived when she'd done all she could, Susan was sure that she'd not be having a bit of trouble with anyone being able to pin this shit on her. Drew was gone and would soon be forgotten, and she'd go back to doing what she wanted from now on.

However, it didn't quite work out the way that she'd hoped it would. She'd been wrong about so many things that day, not thinking beyond getting his body out of the way that those little things haunted her to this day. Fucking little fucker, he should have done just what she wanted, and they'd both have lived for another fight.

Susan still had no idea how they'd figured out that she'd hit Drew's bike. Of course, there had been the damage to her car that she couldn't explain. Also, his bike, which to this day she wished she'd hidden as well—they were able to match her front end to the damage on his bike. Then, there was the blood on her tires, too. All that evidence that said she did it was right there, and no one arrested her. She would never understand why they didn't put her in prison, but she supposed her parents had something to do with that.

Her parents had been paying off people for things that she'd done since she'd been in grade school. After the first couple of times her being able to get away with anything she did, she upped her game. Making a game of being able to get away with…well, murder had been so much fun to her. Then she'd been cut off when they accused her— rightly so, she supposed of killing her cousin.

It wasn't as if Drew was all that special. He was a nice person, she supposed. Not to her. He told her once that he didn't like her at all. Not even a little bit. She didn't care for him either, he was just a fun victim that she could hurt and get away with. However, not Caitlyn. She was meaner than her and could get back at her in ways that would get Susan hurt. A slap to the face when she was out. Tripping her up when she was walking so she'd fall on her face. Little things like that that would ruin her day so that she'd have to hide away until she healed up. It wouldn't have done anything to her reputation if she'd been beaten around by her younger cousin. Not at all.

Just as Susan was headed to the bathroom to clean up, she glanced at the television. It wasn't usually on during meal times, so she was surprised that not only was it on, but a lot of people were staring at it with gaping mouths. It took her a few minutes to realize that not only was it her dad on the set but also her cousin and brother. Terrance was doing the talking at the moment.

"…burial will be after the police have finished doing what they need in order to find the person who killed my younger cousin, Drew Snow, but also who had hidden his body away. Because of where Drew had been hidden in the walls, we've been informed that everything about the murder has been preserved for a look into his death." He pointed out into what Susan could only assume was a crowd of newspaper people. Nodding, her brother answered. "Yes, the police do have a suspect that they're going to be picking up for questioning. As soon as this person is in custody, my family and I think that the case will be solved quickly after that. If you're watching this, whomever killed Drew, your days are numbered, and we will have justice for his death."

Susan thought that Terrance was speaking directly to her with his last sentence. The hair on the back of her neck and arms stood up. Looking around, she wondered if anyone here had remembered that her name was Snow, too. Gathering up her things from her area, Susan was headed out the door when someone called her name.

She didn't stop to see what they wanted. Nor did she bother with trying to ask if she could return tonight. This place was now a place where the police could find her. Going out the door into the slap of cold, Susan knew that she'd be cold for a long time before she felt safe again.

This was going to delay her being able to have the hospital shut down, she was sure. Without a computer that she could email shit out from and the equipment that she'd been using to make it happen, she'd have to do it later. Hopefully, she'd find a place to hide in soon enough.

"Susan Snow." Looking at the officer standing

in front of her, she asked him who he was looking for. "We know who you are, Ms. Snow. If you would just come along quietly, it'll be easier on you."

"What is it you want? I've been staying away from my family. Though I don't have a clue as to why they're doing this to me. I miss them so much. Even my cousin, Caitlyn, though, she's upset with me as well." He asked if it had anything to do with her involvement with Andrew Snow's death. "Why would they think I had anything to do with that? I mean, even the judge said that he didn't think there was enough evidence to convict me for anything. And as far as I know, his body hasn't ever been—"

"They found him yesterday afternoon. It was confirmed with DNA and physical identification that it was his body that was concreted into the walls of the morgue just about an hour ago. We'd been asked to keep an eye on you until we had it confirmed before we were to pick you up for questioning." Susan looked at the distance between her and the alley when the man laughed again. "If you give us any crap or try to run off, we have full authority to shoot to kill. Are you going to run?"

"Christ, all this over a hit and run?" He said he'd not told her that it was a hit and run. "No, you didn't, but I was there for when he came up missing, wasn't I? I remember what was said. And I had nothing to do with it. None of it."

"I guess we'll have to wait and see." She didn't have a choice but to go with the man. As she was being read her rights and cuffed, four more officers pulled up in front of the shelter 'to assist' in her being arrested. Again. "You have any questions?"

"Yes, will I be able to talk to my parents? My brother, too?" He informed her that they didn't wish to talk to her at any time. "Well, that's just mean if you ask me. What happened to innocent until proven guilty? Well? I'm not going to get a fair trial — to find me innocent — if my own family won't support me."

"Not my problem. I was just to bring you in to be questioned. I would tell you not to make any long-term plans if I were you. You just might find yourself having to cancel them." She snarled at him and earned herself a pop with his hand on the back of her head. "You'll behave, Susan Snow, or I'll tape your mouth closed and put you in the trunk to keep you from messing up my newly cleaned car."

The ride from Columbus wasn't that long, but they wouldn't allow her to have a blanket, nor would they let her put on her sweater, all she had to fight the cold. The fuckers were going to pay for their treatment of her, see that they didn't. Then, if how they were treating her wasn't bad enough, he turned up some kind of twangy music loud enough to wake the dead. Christ, she should have taken better care of not being found, she thought.

~*~

While Darrel hadn't been able to do the autopsy on Drew, he was able to be in the room while it had been going on. So long as he didn't comment or ask any questions. He was fine with that. Anything to get this thing ended so that he could go on with his life. He didn't know what his life was going to be about, but it was better than just waiting.

"Doctor Archer, can you come here for a moment?" He told the coroner what he'd been told about helping him out. "Yes, I'm aware of your restrictions, but I have something here that I want you to witness for me. That is allowed."

"All right." He made his way to the table where the young man had been laid out. "What do you have there, sir?"

Even looking at it with a magnifying glass didn't let his mind center on what he was looking at. Pulling on gloves, he was handed the small chain and wiped some of the old dark blood off with them. The bracelet was beautiful, expensive too, if he didn't miss his bet. Several diamonds were in the lettering. However, it was the name 'Susan' written in script that was what was making him second guess himself. To him, it was like she'd left a calling card behind on the body.

"Where was this? I mean, did you pull it off of his wrist or something?" Doctor Wellington told him that it was lying in the cuff of the young man's pants. "I see. I mean, I don't, but...it's evidence, I'd say."

"Yes. There are a couple of more things that I've found while cutting away the clothing. Look at this?" He did when the broken nail was handed to him in a plastic evidence bag. "This was in his skull. I marked the place where it had been protruding from a wound back there. Also, and this is something that I'd not have recognized at all if not for my granddaughter using them, but I do believe that this is a contact lens."

Darrel said that he was going to contact the Feds about this. They had, he'd been told, gone over the body before Wellington had been assigned to do the autopsy. He didn't want to tell them that they missed things, but in order to keep things on the up and up, he knew that if they didn't inform them about it, they'd think that he or Wellington had planted the evidence.

When the Feds entered the room with them, looking over their list of things that had been done to the body, it was discovered that not only had the search of the body been skipped over, even the clothing, but all of it hadn't also been cut away and put into baggies either. Darrel was thrilled to death that he'd had no part in what was going to be a major fuck up if he didn't miss his bet.

It was five hours later before he got back to working on the body on his own. Wellington said that he couldn't do it any longer that his 'worn out body' couldn't stand up that long again. So, with the watchful eye of four FBI agents, he was the coroner in charge of Drew Snow. And he wasn't missing a step by keeping the four people informed of every move he made as well as each and every thing that he found. Which was plenty more than he thought he'd find

In addition to the bracelet and the nail, they found hair consistent with Susan's hair on the clothing. It had been all over the young man's pants that had been taken off by Wellington. The lens was too degraded for DNA, but it did have a manufacturer's number that someone could reference as to who would have had the prescription for it. There were plenty of fingerprints, too, that were lifted. Several were on the zipper of the body bag and even more on the shoe that had been on him when found. When he combed out the hair on the young man, he found a second fingernail as well as about a cup of glass shards that could have come from any number of places on the car that hit him. Darrel was just working on the body when one of the agents spoke to him.

"Does anyone know why she ran him down?" The man standing next to the agent said that they were there not to be the judge. "All right, does anyone know why someone would have allegedly run this young man down?"

"I wouldn't know. And I'm not just covering my butt, but I can't imagine why anyone would want to harm a kid like this one was. According to everyone that we've spoken to, Drew was a polite young man who had a lot going for him." Darrel had heard that as well, mostly from his sister. Drew had been out riding his bike with his friends when the other kids left him to go home. "From what I've gathered, Drew told the others he was heading home to do some homework. He never arrived. Finding his body had been surprisingly easy, I was told. An off-duty officer had come up on the skid marks across his driveway that had just been redone. He thought that his son had made them, so he followed them to find his boy when he came upon Drew. Whoever hit him, whether it had been an accident or not, they left behind the car and the bike as evidence."

Darrel listened to the men with half an ear. He had a job to finish up here, and he didn't want their speculations to taint what he was finding. And he was finding a great deal of evidence that pointed directly at Susan Snow. Forgetting for a moment that he had company in the room, Darrel did what he always did and spoke into the microphone as he did his job.

"Subject was run over at least three, perhaps four times with a car before the person was finished. His legs have been crushed by the tires, as well as his chest. There are markings that I have indicated and photographed. All his ribs were broken or shattered as well." One of the men stepped back from the table. "I'm sorry. I record my findings and then put them on paper later. If you wish, I can—"

"No, you do what you need to do. This is a little more than I bargained for, I guess. Just to know that someone deliberately ran over him several times makes my belly lurch. I have a son about this young man's age. It's disturbing to me to know that there are people out there like this, I guess." The agent laughed a little, but it didn't sound like he was thinking it was funny. "I guess in my line of work, you'd think that I'd be used to this. But not this. I don't want to ever get used to seeing something like this."

"I don't blame you. It would make you mad, I think, to see something like this happen to someone so young and not be fazed by it. I know it happens to me every time I have to preform one of these." The first agent asked him how long he'd been doing autopsies. "Five years. When it became apparent that I'd be able to work with the police more if I was qualified to help them out on occasion, I went back to school to be a certified medical examiner. Then while there, I heard that they had forensic analysis classes that would help me in identifying things on a body that I might well have missed. It has served me very well."

Darrel was there for another four hours before he was finished. Mostly, it was because he was having to mark and bag things that he found. A bit of paint on Drew's shirt. There had been burn marks from tires on his legs. Even taking pictures of the bruising had taken a great deal of his time. It seemed to him that he'd been sorely abused before he'd died.

The agents with him asked him questions too that he had to answer. They were good questions, but they took time out of his work to give them the answers. He was sure that they needed them, the answers for the upcoming trial, but for now, he just wanted them to leave him alone so that he could go home. Exhaustion had been wearing him down for the last hour of working.

The body of Drew was put back in one of the coolers when he'd finished. Darrel had marked all the items as to where they were found and their weight. Usually, on a body that died at home, he would have as many as four baggies of things found. With Drew, he had well over six hundred baggies of found things, and he didn't know if he might have missed one or two. Stretching out his body as he made his way to the upper floor, he was startled to see Caitlyn there, sleeping on a couple of chairs that had been shoved together. There was no way that she was comfortable. He went to reception to find out how long she'd been there.

"Since you got here, I think. She spoke with

your mother for a little while and then asked if she could wait on you. You're to wake her up if you can. She's aware that you were doing the autopsy and has been warned you couldn't tell her anything. The poor lamb. The two of you should go and get you some breakfast. That'll be good for the two of you." He asked her if she was playing matchmaker. "No. Though she seems like a good girl. Your momma has taken a shine to her." Carol snapped her fingers. "I have a message for you. They've brought in Susan Snow for questioning. From what I've heard, she's saying that she hasn't any idea what everyone is talking about. She's been tried once for his death. How does that work?"

"I haven't any idea. That would be a question for one of my brothers. Peter would be the best bet in knowing it, however." She nodded, and he made his way over to where Caitlyn was sleeping. It made him smile when she snored just a little. Touching his fingers to her cheek, which looked so wonderfully soft, she stared up at him with a huge smile on her face. "A person could easily get used to seeing you waking up next to you, I think. Especially if you're going to smile at them like that. Would you like some breakfast with me?"

"Yes." He knew that he had flustered her. He was sort of himself. "I do need to find a restroom first. Is that all right?"

"Sure. They're just over there." He couldn't help but watch her as she made her way to the ladies' room. When she came back, picking up a duffle that was under the chairs she'd been sleeping in, she mentioned that she was going to brush her teeth, too. Darrel leaned back in the chair next to her bed and thought about the dangerous fires he was creating for himself.

This was just what he didn't want to happen. Someone to come around, and he'd be the next son to be married—the last one to marry. His mind, as it usually did when he was alone, drifted to how beautiful Caitlyn was and how much she seemed opposed to being hitched up as he was. But she was beautiful and seemed to have her head on straight.

When she came back from the bathroom, he stood up and put out his arm to escort her out. She asked him where they were going, and all he could think about was going to his apartment, eating a bowl of bad for him cereal, and going to bed. But smiling at her, he asked her if she wanted a carb-filled bad for you breakfast or go someplace where it would be semi-healthy.

"Carbs. And a little bit of good stuff. I like fruit." He told her he did as well, and they headed to the cafeteria after asking her if that was all right. "Perfect. I could eat a horse and drink enough water to float away on."

"Sounds delicious." In the end, they both got a plate of different things to share and talk. Darrel was happy that she didn't bring up her brother and that the conversation was good. He thought that he could talk to her all day about nothing at all and be happy. Yes, he thought, he was on dangerous grounds here.

Chapter 4

Susan waited in line to use the phone like the others were. She didn't care for it, not at all, but that was the rules. Not that she would normally follow the rules if she didn't have to, but the cop that was watching her had his hand on his gun, and she'd been warned — several times now that she doesn't make the rules, but she was going to follow them. Fuckers.

When it was finally her turn, she made the call that she knew would solve everything. When her dad answered the phone, she told him that she'd been arrested and that she needed him to come and bail her out. She was his daughter, after all.

"No." She waited for him to say he was kidding when the line went dead. He'd hung up on her. Christ, she didn't know what to do so she started to call him back. However, she wasn't able to due to the fact that she was only allowed one phone call and she'd had it.

"But the connection was lost. That isn't right. I need to call him back so that he can talk to me." She was told to go to the back of the line. "You're not listening to me. I need to call him back. Something went wrong, and the connection was lost."

"It sounds like your problem. Go to the back of the line now, or I'm going to put you there." She glared at the man standing there until he laughed. "I have four teenage daughters. You looking at me like that doesn't even phase me. Get to the back of the line, as I said, or I'm going to put you there."

She didn't like it, but she did it. Hopefully, Dad was making arrangements to come here and get her out of this mess. Surely he couldn't be still pissed off at her for killing Drew. Christ, that was old news. He was dead. Who cared?

Once she was back at her cell—there couldn't have been a more appropriate name for the place she was in, she decided that her dad was going to have to come up with a plan, or she was going to have to take care of him too. Just as she was thinking that everyone needed to pay for her being arrested, she was told she had a visitor.

"Finally." She did as she was told and moved to the back of her cell. "Will I need to bring anything with me? I mean, I do have a couple of things here that I need when I get out."

"You have a visitor, inmate, not a way out of here. I've told you this several times: you're not going to be set free. Your court hearing is set for tomorrow morning, and you'll be here until judgment is made against you." She told him she wanted out of here. "Well, isn't that too bad? You want to see your visitor or not?"

"Yes. Christ, you people drive me crazy." She had to be handcuffed and shackled. Like there was any way that she could run right now. As she made her way to a room, she asked who it was that was there to see her. Not one answer or hint as to who was coming. "It had better be my dad. He's supposed to be bailing me out."

The officer didn't say a word back to her, and that pissed her off. As soon as her hands were locked to the table and her legs to the floor, the officer stood back from her. His hand on his gun was supposed to be some kind of warning, she was sure, but she didn't get it. They didn't have shit on her after all this time, and she wasn't going to be staying here that much longer.

"Hello, Susan." She nearly stood up and would have if not for being locked down. She'd not seen her brother in years since he'd been working abroad for so long. "You look like you belong here. I hope you're getting used to being behind bars and locked up all the time."

"Did you bring the money that I'm going to need to get out of here, Terrance? I'm sick of being accused of something that I didn't do." He said that he was here on behalf of his parents. "They're my parents too, dumbass. If you don't have money for me, then I have no reason to speak to you."

"That's fine by me. Because I do want to speak to you about the shit that is going on about you. I could give you the rundown of what people are saying about you. Or not. I don't care if you understand that you're not getting out. I think you might have heard it all before. You've never been a nice person, have you, Susan? However, I'm thinking that you've known that for a good long time. But moving on. They've found Drew's body. I think you were told that. And there is so much evidence that puts you at the crime scene that it's going to be hard for you to keep saying you didn't kill him. Everyone knows that you did it." She snorted at him and told him that she didn't care. "You should. Anyway, Dad sent me here to tell you not to call home again. He's not going to bail you out. And when you do go to prison, none of us will come and see you either. Not until you're dead, and that would only be to make sure that you are. You've really fucked up this time, Susan."

"I don't know what you're talking about." He smiled at her, but it was far from congenial. "Why isn't Dad bringing me any bail money? I know that the trial is tomorrow morning but he can at least start greasing palms now. It's the least he can do as he's not raised a hand to help me since this shit hit the newspaper."

"The least he can do is what he is currently doing. Ignoring your demands for bail money on the grounds that he no longer has you as a daughter." She said that she was his daughter. "You have been stricken from the will, Susan. As well as anything else that makes you seem like a part of our family. Mine, Mom and Dad's family. Then there is Caitlyn. Did you know that she's been advocating for you to be put into the worst kind of prison? I'd say that's about right since you did murder her brother. Why did you do it? What did he ever do to you that would make you run over him several times before kidnapping his body and hiding it away? He was a great kid."

"That's what everyone says. Drew was so nice. He was so smart. Well, if he was so smart, why did someone kill him?" Terrance asked her why she'd killed him. "Maybe he said something to me. Maybe he told me no. You know how much I hate that word."

Susan was happy to see him touch the scar she'd given him above his brow when she'd thrown a hanger at him. She had frisbeed it across the room at him, hoping to catch him in the throat when he'd told her no. Again, she didn't remember why he'd said that to her or what she had wanted. But it was good that he remembered what she could do when someone said that to her. When he stood up, Susan told him to sit his ass down.

"Still ordering people about like you have a right to do, aren't you, Susan? Well, I've grown up and come to realize that you're a fucking cunt, and I don't have to listen to you anymore." She told him he was wrong and thanked him for calling her a cunt. "You would think that was something special, wouldn't you. Well, I'm finished with you. I'll be at the trial tomorrow, but I'll be sitting with *my* parents and Cailyn. You can rot in hell for all I care about you."

After she was alone in the room but for the cop, she screamed out her frustrations as loud and long as she could. Hoping for some kind of reaction from someone, anyone, she was left feeling so disappointed that she wanted to scream again. Susan couldn't understand why everyone was against her all of a sudden when any time before Drew was dead, they'd be all over themselves trying to make things right for her.

Being escorted back to her cell, Susan tried to think what she was supposed to do now. Without her parents there to bail her out, she didn't have much recourse other than to go to the stupid trial and worm her way out of it from there. Surely, they didn't think that once she was out, and they had nothing on her to say differently, she wouldn't retaliate against them for their treatment of her, did they?

When she was in her cell, she decided that she needed to make a list of things that she knew would get Terrance and her mother in trouble. Demanding a sheet or two of paper to write things down with a pen, she was told that she wasn't allowed any extras.

"Paper and pen isn't extra dumbass but

essential for my wellbeing. And yours if you don't get your ass in gear and get it for me. Christ, I hate you all right now." The officer walked away. Another thing that she despised more than the word no was having someone ignore her in favor of walking away. "Did you hear me? I want paper and pen so that I can make a list."

"No." Susan's head felt like it was going to explode when the cop told her that. Before she could scream at him for talking to her that way, she heard the big door to this part of the jail slam shut. It was all she could do not to shake the bars loose so that she could make a point.

Susan wondered if she could sue her parents for telling her they weren't going to help her. They'd been doing it all her life, and it was unfair of them to stop just because…well, she didn't know why they were stopping it now, but it was completely unfair of them to do it. Then she remembered that two days ago, she'd fired her attorney.

He wasn't worth shit anyway, the way he kept telling her that she should just take what the state was offering her and not get the death penalty. Like that was going to happen. She figured that she would represent herself in this shame of a trial, and that would be her best bet of getting out. Since her parents weren't going to fork over any money or support to their own child, no less, then she was going to have to take matters into her own hands. Susan laid back on her cot and thought about what she was going to do when she first got out.

"Other than kill everyone that has been around me for the last two weeks." She thought about Caitlyn, too. It was all her fault that she wasn't free. Not that she had ever done anything to her other than to ignore her, Susan still hated her.

Caitlyn had been smarter and much prettier growing up than Susan had been. She dated more often, too. Her dresses, too, were so much prettier. Not that she'd ever tell Caitlyn her thoughts on her. Not once in all their growing up had Caitlyn ever done one thing for her that she'd wanted. Not even to ask her to go on some of her family vacations with her either.

Not that dating had been anything that she liked when she'd been living at home. Of course, no one asked her out. Not even the worst-looking guy at school would ask her to go to her prom. So she went alone and made it hard on every person that she thought should have at least asked her. Hard in the way that she had embarrassed them until they left. Oh, to be in high school again, she thought.

She must have dozed off at some point. The only way that she could sleep on this lumpy bed was to be exhausted when someone said her name to wake her. Sitting up, she asked the cop standing there what the hell he wanted. At his grin, she knew that whatever it was, she wasn't going to be happy about it.

"You want a shower?" She told him, again, that she only took showers in the morning. So her hair wouldn't be a mess first thing. "You either take it now, or you'll go to the hearing the way you are."

"Then I'll go the way that I am." She was given another jumper to wear tomorrow. "Where are my clothes that I came in here with? Or contact my parents to have them bring me something to wear. That's the one thing that I remember from that lawyer guy was that I could wear my own clothing to the trial."

"I asked your brother while he was here. He told me that his family—he made it quite clear that I understood that they were his family had gutted your room to the walls and had it redone when you murdered their nephew. Nothing of you is left in the house, he said. Oh, if it were that easy to get rid of you from here." She told him that it wasn't possible that they'd do that to her. "And yet it is possible. I believe now that I think on it, they gave all your clothing to the local homeless shelter so that other people might find some use of your crap."

"You're a liar." The officer asked her if she called everyone that when they said something to her that they didn't like. "In this, I know that you're a liar. They'd not do that to me. I'm their daughter."

"You *were* their daughter. I believe once they got a restraining order against you, they cut you off at the knees. Then, when Mr. Snow put in the paper not long after Drew was murdered that he was no longer responsible for you nor your debts, that he was no longer your father." He laughed. "Let me ask you something, Susan, have you ever been a nice or even a good person? From where I'm standing, on this side of the bars, I don't think so. I remember you as a child. You were a horrific person even then."

"I had fun. There was nothing wrong with someone having fun, was there? I don't think you being on that side of the bars is all that special if you ask me. Did you ever have fun, Carter? I mean, with your family being so fucking poor, I don't know how you could. Christ, when I think of you in high school, it's a small wonder that any of you guys in that family survived, what with the way your father drank all the time. Didn't he beat you kids too?"

"He did. Momma, too, if you didn't know that. But then he won the lottery with my mom, and everything changed for him and us. Did you know that, Susan? That my family is richer than yours is now. Dad not only got himself sobered up, but he didn't have to work anymore, either. He made up for the treatment of us tenfold by being a good father and grandfather to our kids. He does charitable work all the time. And he's a better man for it. What do you have to show for you having had money? Nothing, that's what. You're still behind bars, and no one likes you any more than they did when you were a kid." She asked him how he figured that his family was richer than hers was. "Because we're all together and are glad to be so. Love and friendship are what keep us happy. Not that you have any of that either."

"You're full of shit." Susan turned her back on Carter. "There is no way that you have more money than I do."

"Than you do? That's easy. You don't have anything now, do you? Not even family helping you through this terrible time in your life." He was still laughing when he walked away from her. She screamed at him about her clothing, and he laughed all the harder.

"Mother fucker. They're all going to pay for this. I don't know how, but I'm going to see what I can do."

Once the lights were out, Susan had a mental list of things that she was going to do. However, while sitting in the dining area tonight, she got a glimpse of the news that was on the television. There was a hell of a crowd out by the courthouse, and people were holding up signs that said she should fry. Not the kind of things that made her think that she was going to get one bit of sympathy when she started talking about how she'd been innocently accused of killing her cousin. She needed a better plan, she told herself. And less than ten hours to come up with one. Christ, she hated what she'd been reduced to of late.

~*~

Darrel knew that he was going to have to testify as a witness, but for now, he was just as happy sitting with his family in the courtroom. Since Susan had been arrested, lots of things that he'd been worried about were coming out all right on his end.

The hospital was safe now from not just being

closed down but torn down as well. Thus, his job. The Feds had been able to nail down where the emails were coming from and had been able to put a stop to the rumors of the hospital being torn down to rest. It had a bouncer—a program that would make the IP address jump from computer to computer- but it always ended up at the one at the grocery store where Caitlyn worked.

The men who had come out to x-ray the walls had found a couple of places that needed to be reinforced in the walls at the hospital, for which everyone was grateful to have found and that had been taken care of by his family. All good news on that front, he knew.

Darrel knew that he'd slept better last night than he had since he'd gotten the first email. Glancing at Cailyn, who he'd been spending a lot of time with, he thought she'd had a great deal to do with him feeling better. Darrel couldn't understand now that he'd been hanging out with her why he'd been so opposed to having her as a friend. She was all that and more to him, he thought. Not that they were even close to the point of dating. If they ever were, he thought.

Del sat down next to him, on the opposite side

that Caitlyn was sitting on, and smiled at him. Waiting for the judge to come in and get things started, his brother said hello to Caitlyn, then frowned at him.

"What's the matter?" He asked Del what he meant. "You have the goofiest smile on your face. You're not going insane, are you? Or are you in love? That's what I said, but Merce assured me that's not it."

"I'm not in love." He'd said it so loud that several people turned and looked at him. Lowering his voice again, he told him that he wasn't in love. "We're just friends if you're referring to Caitlyn." They both glanced at her when she said they were just friends. "See? Just friends."

"Okay, okay. You don't have to keep telling me." He thought that, apparently, he did since he was still grinning at him like a loon. "You do know that's the way it starts out. Just being friends."

"Oh, do shut up." Mom popped Del on the back of the head, and he couldn't help but laugh. "See, even Mom knows that we're just friends. Stay out of it Del. Not everyone has to be as happy as the rest of you are. I can have friends all I want and never get married."

"I don't want to marry either. There is just too

much…do you have any idea how much work it takes for people to get married and live happily ever after? More work than I want to invest in things." Caitlyn looked at him and smiled. "You're a good friend, Darrel, and I couldn't be happier with saying that to you. I don't want anything else from you but friendship. Ever."

For some reason, it hurt him a little that she said it like that. Ever? She didn't want anything from him ever? Letting it go as best he could, Darrel paid attention to the proceedings going on in front of him. Once the judge was finished telling the jury why they were there and the rules, Susan stood up when asked to do so. She looked terrible. Which he supposed was the way it should have been. She'd been in jail for about three weeks now.

"Where is your attorney, Ms. Snow? I'm sure that one was assigned to you." She told the judge that she was going to represent herself in this. "This is a murder trial, young lady, and I won't have you coming back on me or anyone else saying you were foolhardy in thinking that you could do this on your own." He turned to the bailiff. "Go out into the hall and find me one for her. Not an Archer, however, that would be the best she'd ever get, but someone that isn't related to this trial at all."

The bailiff came back almost twenty minutes later, saying that they had scattered like the wind as soon as he'd opened the door. Peter, who was working for the Snow family, barely seemed to hide his mirth, but one hard glance from the judge and he turned it into a cough.

"Well, I'm not going to allow this woman to do a crappy job here and blame it on her lack of representation. I'll be back." Everyone stood up as soon as he did, but he was in his office before anyone could say anything. Susan kept yelling that she didn't want an attorney. Darrel was positive that if Susan didn't shut up before he returned, she was going to end up on the wrong end of the judge. Since she was already in deep water with him, he might well just send her back to her cell and let her find out her fate from them. Christ, she was loud.

It was about ten minutes later when he joined them again. It was beginning to look like a jack in the box in the courtroom, the way that they kept bouncing up and down. He informed them that an attorney was coming in shortly and that he didn't want to hear another word from Susan. Of course, that didn't shut her up. It wasn't until he threatened her with going back to jail that she seemed to understand who was in charge. At least, he thought she did. She had a way about her that made people want to smack her around a little.

As soon as the attorney showed up, still dressed in jeans and a shirt that things started up for the trial. He had an hour to go over the paperwork on the trial before it began, and the judge, Judge Holdom, he found out, called lunch. Darrel just wanted this over with, and all these delays were stressing him out. He was glad for Caitlyn's company to sit with him so that he could vent a little. His family went home to check on things there while he stayed for his part in the trial.

"You're going to be all right, aren't you? My dad died from too much stress, and you look to be a single heartbeat from having a stroke. Just chill the fuck out before I have to hit you." Taking her hand into his, he kissed the back of it and told her that he was trying. "Well, try harder. I don't want to have to figure out what to do with your body when your family finds out."

"Yeah, I think that they would be upset with me. It's been difficult the last few months. Everything has come out on top in the end, but it just seems that more and more shit keeps getting piled up on other shit until you don't think there is a light at the end of the tunnel." He stretched his neck and sat up straighter in the chair. "All right. I'm feeling better. I just want to get my part over with and not screw things up for either of our families. You've no idea how much I don't like having to go to court on things like this."

"You'll do fine. I know it." They nibbled around on their sandwiches before Caitlyn spoke again. "Why is it you're so opposed to marriage? You can tell me it's none of my business if you want."

"It's not marriage that I'm opposed to but the timing." She cocked her brow at him. "Like I said, there is so much going on. I know that my brothers are all thrilled to have someone in their lives who loves and holds them. But I don't think that there is anyone out there for me that would be just as understanding and all right with me having to get up in the middle of the night. Sometimes, as many as four times in a week. That would be rough on anyone."

"I don't know. It's not like the person that you're leaving in that nice warm bed has to get up and go with you. But I guess I can see where some women would be like that. Even during the day, you'd have to be prepared to do your job even if you've other plans." He told her that was it exactly. And having children would be worse, he told her. "Yes. Birthday parties would have to be planned around that happening. Holidays as well. I would imagine that you could carve out some time for vacations. Someone could take over for you if you were to want some time away with your family. Right?"

"Yes, that would be easy enough, I guess. I mean, I've covered for nearly everyone in the hospital at least a couple of times when they had vacation time coming." He thought of the doctors that he had worked for. "They sure do put everything into those vacations when they take them. One year I worked for an entire month for a doctor while she took her family on a long cruise, stopping in about every port they came to. She said that she wanted to do that every year. I think she has, too."

"That would be a blast. Taking a family on a long cruise and having fun. I've always wanted to go to Alaska to see the whales. Also, around Europe. Have you ever been?" He said that he'd taken two weeks off just a few months ago to do just that. "I bet that was fun for you. Getting to go on things at your own pace. I'd like that. It's why I don't care for guided tours anywhere. I want to stop and read the information that is out there. See all that I can."

Darrel thought of the families that he encountered while on his latest vacation. He found himself following them around a little just to hear the kids' excitement about some of the places they were at. Even the youngest child, no more than about four, had her own camera and was taking pictures of her first real vacation. Her mother had told Darrel that she was going to print every picture and put it in an album so she'd have it when she was older. Or perhaps taking her own family on the same vacation. He loved that idea.

Finishing off their lunch, he met his family in front of the courthouse when they arrived. Getting hugs from the kids, something that he loved very much, the adults went into the courthouse while the kids were going to go to the indoor gym/playground to have some fun. He couldn't imagine them not being bored to death sitting in their family. Not to mention, when he got up to testify, what they'd think about how badly the young man had been hurt. He himself had a few nightmares when he thought about how much Drew had suffered at the hands of someone else.

While Judge Holdom spoke to the attorney for Susan, David Stockley, Susan was told to keep her mouth shut as many as ten times. Finally, he gave her a choice. She either shut up, or he was going to have her taken back to her cell for the remainder of the trial. Which could be, he told her, as much as six months.

Darrel didn't see that, but it had the desired effect. She not only kept her mouth shut, but she was no longer bitching to Stockley about how much she did not want him around. Darrel also knew that this was going to be hard on the man, not having much time to go over the information that he'd been given. But Darrel also had an idea that Peter, the attorney for the other side, would cut him some slack, too. Everyone, it seemed to him, wanted this thing over with. And with Susan paying for her crimes against Drew.

There was also the upset at the hospital, but he was all right with having that put on the back of her trial over the murder of her cousin. It was all taken care of now; the hospital was taking care that any of the false information about its closing was gone or had been taken care of. Ads had been taken out in newspapers across the country, and he was glad too that other than a few people still worried about it, they'd found a way for it to never happen again by putting out reports monthly to tell how well the hospital was doing.

Chapter 5

Caitlyn watched Darrel as he told the jury his findings on Drew's body. It hurt her in ways that she couldn't imagine to think how much he'd suffered before dying. And even after he was dead, he'd been abused so badly that it was difficult for her to think that any human being could have done that to someone, much less someone as nice as her brother had been.

He wasn't perfect. But he was her brother, and she could overlook some of his teenage shit when it came to him being the youngest of the two of them. It hurt her how much she missed him every minute of every day.

When Darrel was finished, she looked at the photos that had been up on the retractable shade they were using as a viewing tool. It made her ill to think that these things had been done to Drew, but he was finally getting justice, and that was wonderful. Darrel was cross-examined then, and she paid attention to the attorney to see what kind of questions he had for Darrel.

"You're Doctor Darrel Archer, is that correct?" Darrel said that was him. "It says here that you have been okayed by not just the president of the United States but also the Vice President too to work in any hospital across the country. Is that correct?"

"It is." Holdom asked him how that qualified him as a Medical Examiner in this case. "I have a doctorate in medicine as well as a medical degree to be a physician. In addition to that, I have additional residency training in forensic pathology and a forensic pathology fellowship with Doctor Wellington as a certified medical examiner. I'm working on my doctorate in becoming a medical examiner to take over when Dr. Wellington retires in a few years. He's been asking me to take over his work more and more as he gets older. I thought it best that I know all that I needed to know in the event I am accepted into that job."

After a few more questions about his qualifications, Stockley asked him about the wounds that had been marked on Drew's body that pertained to him being run over by a car more than one time.

"The tire impression is there on the picture. I can tell that the person or persons that ran over Mr. Snow had stopped at the midpoint to his chest and then back up. The same impressions are reversed several times, crushing his ribs and having, at one point, several pieces of chest and rib bone puncturing not just his lungs, making it nearly impossible for Mr. Snow to breathe, but also I found fragments of bone in his heart as well." He asked how long Mr. Snow lived like that. "Not long. Several minutes is all, but he would have been unable to take a breath as he bled out internally. Even had he been in a hospital when this happened to him, there would have been no saving him as it happened that quickly. However, I'm sure that it felt like forever for the young man struggling to take his last breaths."

Caitlyn looked at Susan and was disturbed that she was smiling like the idea that Drew had suffered so much was funny to her. Shivering when Susan looked her way, Caitlyn reached for something to hold onto when her cousin winked at her. Christ, she was going to be ill.

Looking at the hand that she was holding

onto tightly, she was not surprised to see that it was Darrel's granddad. He'd been keeping an eye on her since Darrel had asked him to. Making sure she was safe when she stepped outside and was there for her when she came and went to the bathroom. Leaning her head on his shoulder, he handed her his handkerchief, a clean one, he assured her when she felt the tears rolling down her face.

When Darrel stood up to come back to his seat, she stood as well and took his hand into hers. She didn't know what she had been planning when she took him out of the courtroom, but she needed to get away from all of it and all the people around. As soon as they were in the hall, Darrel took the lead and led her down the hallway. Once they were at one of the smaller single doors, he pulled her inside and pressed her against the door, taking her mouth with his own.

She didn't have any idea where they were or what was going to happen from them being in a maintenance closet. But as soon as Darrel rolled his hips, pressing his hard cock into her soft folds, she had to have him. Even stripping off her clothing by tearing at them could she think beyond having him fuck her. As soon as she had her blouse off, he ripped her bra open in the front and took her nipple into his mouth. When he sucked hard on her, she cried out and curled her fingers into his hair.

"Christ, yes." She felt her body tighten when he suckled hard. As soon as he wrapped his hands around her ass cheeks and pulled her up, he entered her pussy so quickly that it took her breath away by his size. Screaming around his mouth on hers, Caitlyn came three times, one right after the other, so quickly that she was hard-pressed to catch her breath. When he lifted his head from her breast, she stared at him as he fucked her slowly.

Moving in and out of her, she watched his face. He did the same to her as she held onto his shoulders. He begged her to feed him, and letting go of his arms, she lifted her breasts up to his mouth until he could taste her. Caitlyn held his mouth to her as she closed her eyes. Every time his cock filled her, filling her fully when he buried his cock to his balls deep inside of her body seemed to scream for more. For him to never stop what he was doing until they were one.

"I love you." She looked up at him when he said that to her — screamed it at her as it turned out while he was coming deep inside of her for the first time. "I love you more than I ever thought possible."

"Oh, Darrel, I don't think I could ever love anyone but you." It occurred to her in that moment that she did indeed love him. And had since she'd met him. Holding onto him, he took her, pressing her even harder against the door to where they were. Things on the walls shook off their hooks. The shelf that was next to them rattled, and things began to shatter on the floor. Almost as soon as he told her again that he would love her forever, he came.

Holding onto Darrel, she felt his cum filling her like he'd been heating her from the inside out. Even her nipples burned with it. As her body began to build up, ready for her own release, Caitlyn closed her eyes and threw back her head. Whatever happened, she could only hope that she lived through it.

The climax was nothing like she'd ever had before. Caitlyn was positive, too, that she'd never have another one like it for as long as she lived. Then she wondered if they'd make love like this all the time, sure that it would kill her and him if they did. Digging her nails into his shoulder, he took her mouth harshly. Tasting a little of her blood when he dipped his tongue into her mouth, it sent a jolt of pleasure through her body that had her screaming out again and again.

Limp, she could barely stand when Darrel set her on her feet. He didn't seem to be doing much better as he was holding onto the now-emptied shelf beside them.

"Do you think they'll make us replace everything in here? I think we broke about four bottles of that deep cleaner." They both laughed as she bent over and picked one of the intact ones up from the floor. While bent, she asked Darrel what this had meant to him.

"Everything. It meant the world to me." He had his back turned to her when she stood up. "I suddenly needed a connection to someone. Someone alive and full of life. I know that it sounds crazy, but all I could think about when I dragged you out of the courtroom was that I was going to die if I didn't touch you. It had to be only you, Caitlyn. I've fallen in love with you. As I said, and I think that for the rest of my life, you will be my only sanity when I feel the way that I did."

"So you're saying I'm a foundation for you to be safe and secure. Is that it?" He turned so quickly that she took a step back from him. "I didn't mean to make you upset with me, Darrel. I just—"

"But Caitlyn, you *are* my foundation. Not

just for me to be safe and secure, as you said, but for my love for you. You're my everything. My all. I didn't…before I met you, I thought—no, I knew that I didn't want a wife. Didn't want a family around me so that I'd not have to divide my time, the little that I have left between you and my work. But I was ever so wrong about it." He growled. "I'm not doing this right. Let me start again. With you and your love, Caitlyn, I feel like the world has opened for me. My heart is full and beating like it has never done before. I feel, honey, you make me feel everything. The air that comes into my lungs. The way my heart beats now that you are a part of it. You mean so much to me. I don't know that if I were to tell you every minute of every day for the rest of my life that I love you, would it ever be enough."

"Oh, Darrel, that's the sweetest thing anyone has ever said to me." Darrel held her to him then, holding her to his heart so that she could hear it beating. His heart beat for her. "I love you so much. With all that I am."

They started out of the closet, and he realized that they were in a state of undress that would get them both arrested, and she had to giggle. Their clothing was a mess. She couldn't find his tie. Even finding the light switch to where they were didn't help them. If she could just stop laughing, she would have been more helpful, but Darrel was laughing just as hard.

When they were decent enough to come out of the closet, he stepped out first. Darrel told her that when the coast was clear, he'd knock on the door for her. Then, once she counted to three, she was to come out with him and act like nothing had happened.

Just as she started to exit the little room, only getting it partly opened, the door hit her on the forehead when it was closed on her again. She wasn't sure what was going on, so she tried to open it again when it hit her in the nose this time. Pushing hard against it, thinking the stupid thing had gotten something stuck, Cailyn fell out of the door and right onto the floor where Darrel and Terrance were. Christ, she was so embarrassed that she couldn't look either man in the face.

"I had something wrong with my dress." Terrance laughed, and she glared up at him as he helped her up from the floor. "You want me to punch you in the face? I said I had something wrong with my dress, and that's what it was."

"I see. Well, I don't know what was wrong

with it before, but now it's inside out. Do you need more help? I can watch the bathroom door while Darrel gets you adjusted — or has he already adjusted you enough, love?" Caitlyn wasn't in the mood. Being this embarrassed was something new to her. Gathering up her purse and her shoes, she made her way down the hall — alone — while Terrance laughed. She was going to kill him. "Caitlyn? Do you need some adjustments? I think Darrel could help you."

Her dress was indeed inside out. Also, the zipper was broken, and she couldn't seem to figure out how to get the stupid button at the top of the sucker inside the smallest button hold she'd ever seen. Giving up on it, knowing that she was making matters worse, she went into the hallway with her sweater that she'd brought with her on, and her hair pulled back in a sloppy ponytail. Terrance was standing outside the room waiting for her.

"One word, and I'll hit you." He smiled at her. When it slipped away, she moved close enough to him to put her hand on his arm. "What is it? Something has happened. Is it your mom? Your dad?"

"Your mom." She braced herself for whatever he was going to tell her. "She made a call to my dad this morning. She wants to see you. I guess the nursing home said that she'd seen the newspaper and that they hadn't thought of her making any kind of connection to your brother."

"Mom hasn't made a connection to anyone or anything in years, Terrance. You know that as well as I do. What does she want, did she say?" Terrance told her that she only told his dad that she wanted to see her. "I'll go when this is over. Unless she said now."

"Now. I talked to Darrel, who I really like, by the way, and he can't leave in the event the jury has any questions for him. I told him that I'd take you." She nodded. "All kidding aside, Caitlyn, but I'll take you by your place if you want first. I don't know what Aunt Tilly wants, but I'm sure you want to look your best. Congratulations, by the way."

"Thank you. We're still working things out." She hugged him after only taking a few steps towards the front of the building to leave. "I love you, Terrance. This must be just as hard on you as it is on me."

"Thank you for that, but, no, it's not. I've washed my hands of Susan a long time ago. Even before she murdered Drew. You might say that I've never had a sister for as much as I care about her and what she's done." Terrance opened the car door for her, and she entered and buckled up. He continued telling her why he didn't care for his sister when he got in. "When I was five, on my birthday, as a matter of fact, my parents had a party for me. Susan decided that since the party wasn't all about her then no one was going to have a good time. She crushed my cake, smeared it all over me and my friends, then broke every gift by stomping on them so that I couldn't have anything she didn't get. It didn't just happen that one time either. She did it for the next two birthdays as well as Christmas or at any time I was given anything. Even if she got something as well. So, I stopped having parties and being around her. She's a fucking bitch, and I wrote her off years ago. Then, when this came up about Drew, I knew, in my heart and mind, that she'd done it. She's always been like that. A selfish bitch that I won't have anything to do with."

The trip to the nursing home didn't take long. Twenty minutes one way, and they were getting out of the car. Before going into the room, Caitlyn went to the little boutique that was there and picked her mom up a couple of things. One of them being a lovely card and the other a warm pair of slippers.

As soon as she walked into the room, she knew that things had changed for her mom. Not only did she look in her direction when she opened the door, but she smiled at her, too. Getting up, her mom hugged her tightly and asked Terrence if he was all right. Caitlyn didn't know what had happened, but she couldn't have been happier about it.

~*~

Darrel was in the kitchen when Caitlyn was dropped off. He'd spoken to her and Terrance when they'd been on their way home, so he knew that Terrance wasn't staying for dinner with them. Just as he was coming out of the kitchen, he heard her new phone ringing. He'd gotten her one just the other morning so that she could keep in contact with him.

"It's the jail." He took the phone when it was offered and asked her what she wanted him to do with the call. "I don't want to talk to Susan. I don't even want her calling here. She's already filled up Terrance's voicemail box. I don't want to hear her telling me again how much I'm ruining her life by blaming her for Drew's murder. Can you fix it so that her calls are blocked?" Darrel nodded but answered the phone call instead.

"Hello? Yes, this is Darrel Archer. Who is

this?" Once had it on speakerphone, she could hear her cousin telling him that she'd called Caitlyn, not him. "Oh, I'm sorry. Caitlyn and I share everything and that would include phone calls. She doesn't want to speak to you. Not ever again. So if you would please—"

"Fuck you. Tell her I said to get onto the phone right now, or I'm going to kill her. I'm sick of fucking around with her. She needs to get her ass down here and bail me out." Darrel told her that there hadn't been any bail amount set. "So? That doesn't mean she can't pay someone to get me out of here. And I'm sick of being ignored by my family, too. You tell her that I want her to go over and see them and tell them that this is ridiculous that they're treating me this way. All the evidence in the world isn't going to change the fact that I'm still their daughter, and I deserve to be treated better than they have treated me."

"Too bad." Susan didn't say anything when she spoke to her. "No, I'm not going to go to your parents' home. I'm not going to pay anyone for you to be released and—I spoke to my mom today. She told me that you spoke to her when you killed Drew."

Darrel looked shocked, and that was the way

that Caitlyn had felt when her mom told her what Susan had said to her. Darrel sat down on one of the dining room chairs and pulled her to him so that she could sit on his lap. It was then that she spoke to Susan about what she'd been told.

"You called my mom to tell her that Drew wouldn't be coming home ever again, didn't you? You told her that you'd just killed him and that if you were there, she would have run you down as well. Run over you four times back and forth because he told you no when you demanded that he turn over his bike to you so that you could give it to the kid down the street. You'd run over his bike simply because you could. Do you remember that, Susan?" Her laughter made her skin crawl. When she said that she'd forgotten why she'd killed him — then she said she supposedly killed Drew that day. "Then you told her, in great detail, what you'd done to him. How you had crushed his legs by running over him. That while driving over him, you had the best climax that you'd ever had. And that as soon as it was possible, you were going to kill me as well. Because you felt that as her aunt she was lacking in how to pick out gifts for someone like you. She didn't know then, nor does she know to this day what that had to do with the death of her only son."

"She would buy me things that you liked. How stupid is that? I'm not at all like you were. And nor are you anything like me now. You're a cow, Caitlyn. Did you hear me? A cow. But I got the last laugh, didn't I? You're all alone but for you insane mother who couldn't hold a candle to me and my family." Caitlyn looked at Darrel when he pointed to her phone. The *rec* in red flashed at her, and she knew that somehow he'd gotten her phone to record what Susan was saying. "When are you coming here? You'd better make it quick. I have shit to do. And don't forget to tell that Archer family that I'm going to make them pay too for finding your dumbass brother's corpse too. That fucking shit isn't going to be easy on any of you."

"My mother, just as Darrel has recorded everything you said to her that day. She handed the recording over to the police when they got to our house." Susan laughed. "You think that it's funny that she got your confession when you killed Drew?"

"I think that it's funny if you think that anyone will believe your mother. She's been in the loony bin for years. Why on earth would anyone care whatever spilled out of her mouth? And I know you can't use what I'm staying to you now because you didn't ask me if you could record shit. So, I'm going to give you what you want, Caitlyn. Are you recording like you said? I hope so. Caitlyn, I murdered your brother in cold blood. Not only did I do that, but I hid away his body, knowing that no one would dare look for him after all this time, and that would have worked out great for me, too. But then you had to stick your nose in shit that didn't have shit to do with you, and now I'm sitting in a jail cell that I'm going to be getting out of soon. You had better watch out, Caitlyn, my dear cousin. Because I'm going to come for you soon, and I'm going to do worse to you than I did your baby brother."

The line went dead, and she sat there on Darrel's lap. Caitlyn turned in his lap, facing him, and smiled. It was at that moment that she understood what he'd said to her earlier about needing a connection.

~*~

"I want to suck your cock. I don't want you to come quickly, but I do want to taste you." He nodded because he was sure he'd lost all feeling in his head, and speech was impossible. "Will you tell me if I do it wrong?"

He nodded again and put his hand on the

dining room table when she slid off his lap to her knees. He watched as she removed her bra and had to turn slightly to lean against the table or fall. Darrel was sure that when she touched him, whether she wanted him to come or not, he was going to.

He'd left his jacket at work, and his tie had come untied at some point in the morning. He reached up with trembling hands and pulled it free of his shirt and finished unbuttoning his shirt. When she opened his belt and left it hanging, he nearly fell back when she opened the zipper with her teeth.

"Caitlyn, please don't tease me much more. You've no idea how hard this is on me." She smiled at him and pulled his pants down around his thighs along with his boxers with his help. How he was able to help her, he had no idea because he seemed to be running on need instead of instinct. Rubbing her cheek over his length, he nearly tore his shirt in half trying to get loose from it. His cock seemed to leap at her when she licked his heavy vein along his shaft.

Darrel wanted to beg her to touch him, but he wanted her to take her time, too. Every part of him screamed for him to help her move things along, but he couldn't. His mouth was as dry as cock was wet as her tongue seemed to be. He watched as she stared at his cock for several seconds before her tongue came out and licked the very tip. He saw stars. And when she wrapped her mouth around his crown, Darrel cried out suddenly. Christ, her mouth was hot.

Fucking her luscious mouth as gently as he could, Darrel curled his fingers into the back of her head and held her to him. Her tongue danced along his cock with every movement, and every time he was ready to explode into her, she'd move. When she cupped his balls and leaned back, he was on the verge of snarling at her to finish him when he looked at her. There couldn't have been a more beautiful woman in the world than her.

"I want you to fuck me." She stood up, and he reached for her. "Right here on the table from behind. Take me, Darrel. Make me feel like a person. Fuck me until I can't stand, then do it again."

Standing up, he stripped the rest of her clothing off. Stripped is just what he did, too, as he tore at her clothing like it was nothing more than paper. The sound of it, the tearing of the cloth, and her begging him for more nearly sent him over the edge. Christ, he thought, why did he never want this woman as his wife. Then something occurred to him. He did want her to be his wife. Forever.

"Marry me." She turned slightly to look at him, and he smacked her ass. He nearly came all over her pinked-up ass when he saw his handprint there. "Say it, Caitlyn, say that you'll be my wife, and I'll fuck you until we're both lying on the floor unconscious."

"Yes. Yes, I'll marry you. Fuck me, Darrel. Fuck me now." He slammed forward into her pussy from behind. As soon as he was buried up to his balls inside of her, she screamed that she was coming. Almost as soon as he pulled nearly to the tip of him from her, he saw their reflection in the window across from them. It was nearly his undoing when he saw her breasts sway back and forth as he fucked her.

He lost count of the amount of times that she came. Her ass was red now as he'd slapped her none too gently when she came. When her body, spent, slumped over the table, he leaned over her and took her so hard that the chairs on the other side of the table fell over, and the table moved across the room to the wall. As soon as the table stopped moving, Darrel let himself go and cried out loudly and long when he came inside of her.

He must have passed out for a few seconds. Or longer, he wasn't sure. But he was on the floor with Caitlyn lying across him. There was a blanket lying over the two of them, and he wondered how they'd gotten there. Caitlyn looked at him from her position on his chest and smiled.

"You were too heavy, and I rolled you onto the floor. If you have a headache, it's my fault because you hit your head when I got you off me." He asked her if she was all right. "I don't think there are enough words to tell you just how all right I am right now. How are you?"

"As much as I hate to admit it, I think that every part of my body is in pain. But it was so worth it." He pulled her up to him and kissed her on the mouth. "I love you, Caitlyn. So very much. I don't know why I ever thought that I didn't want this kind of love in my life."

"You just had to wait for me to come along, that's all." He agreed with her. "I have to get up. I don't want to, but I need to go to the bathroom, and I think my belly thinks that my throat has been cut. I'm starving."

When she got up, he handed her his shirt that he'd had on. There were only a couple of buttons on it, but there was enough to cover her breasts. Christ, he loved this woman. Pulling on his boxers and nothing else, he headed to the kitchen to find them something to eat. When she joined him in the room, he laid out the fixings for them to nibble on and sat down with her. This was the nicest meal he thought that he'd ever had. Mostly, he thought it had to do with the company.

Darrel was in love. And he was loved back. While he knew that he'd forced her hand into saying that she'd marry him, he decided that he was going to do it properly and get down on one knee. He'd do it as soon as he thought that he'd not need help getting up, he thought with a laugh.

Chapter 6

Susan was confident that things were going to go her way this morning. This was the third day in a row that she'd been brought here, and she was no closer to getting out than she'd been the first day. She just wanted to get home and back to her normal life. But today was the day she was going to make them get their shit together and let her go.

Her attorney, the useless piece of shit, told her over and over that she would be better served if she would allow him to bargain with the other side in getting only life in prison without parole. He said that she might get a couple of perks to help her out while in prison. No way, she'd told him. She was *not* going to spend the rest of her life in prison. Not any more time than she already had if she could help it. Fuck this shit. She needed to get out and resume her life the way that she wanted. And fuck that shit about her being on death row too. She had done nothing wrong that they could prove. At least she didn't see where they had anything to make her look like she was guilty.

Susan also wanted to know where in the hell her parents and brother were. They'd not been here one time, nor had let her know either the reason that they weren't coming. Dumbass Stockley kept telling her that she needed to look like she had family support and that they not being there was making her look bad. The only family that was there was her cousin, and she certainly wasn't going to support her in any way that would help her.

As soon as the judge asked if there were any questions, she put her hand up. Stockley tried twice to put it back down, but she finally had to smack him in the face before he left her alone. But the judge asked her what she was doing.

"I don't want to have this all dragged out any more than I—" He told her that she'd made it clear that she didn't want to be there, but why did she smack her attorney. "Oh, I'm forever having to keep him in line. The dumbass wants me to plea bargain when they don't have anything on me."

"So you hit him?" Susan didn't understand why he seemed so shocked by that and shrugged. "Mr. Shockley, in all the last three days, how many times has she hit you? And why haven't you told me about it?"

"I put a detailed letter on your desk just yesterday when I'd had enough. Not only is Ms. Snow physically abusive but verbally as well. Since you demanded that I represent her, I thought that I'd had no choice in what she did to me and would have to suck it up, as she is so fond of telling me to do." Stockley was making a big deal out of nothing, and she told him that. "I have never hated working for a client as much as I have you, Ms. Snow. You are by far the most horrific person that I have ever met."

"Well, la-de-da for you. Christ, you'd think that I took out a ball bat and hit you with it. I haven't yet. Just remember that dumbass." He started to unbutton his shirt, and she stood up the best that she could. "Are you still going to go on about that again? I told you I'd pay for the emergency room visit when I get out of here."

When he pulled his shirt up and over his head and turned his back to the judge, she rolled her eyes. It wasn't really that big of a deal. All she'd done was stab him in the back with his ink pen a few times when he turned his back on her. She'd told him no less than five times that she hated when people did that to her. It was, she knew his fault for not taking her seriously enough.

"Good Christ." The judge came down from his high chair, what she'd been calling his area, and looked at the wounds. Now that she could see them without all the blood from yesterday, Susan knew that she'd gotten him a few more times than she'd thought. It looked sort of — "Ms. Snow, you did this to this man? For what reason would you have to hurt someone this much when it's in your best interest to make sure that you stay at least on his good side. Darrel? Are you here? Can you have a look at this man so that I can document it for the courthouse records?" Susan rolled her eyes before speaking.

"It's not that big of a deal. I did warn him about turning his back on me. That's about the rudest thing someone can do to another person. Then, when he decided to leave me hanging, not that I think he's doing all that much for me in the first place, but he was leaving, and I wasn't finished talking to him yet." The judge asked her about the officer in the room. "Oh, he stepped out when I told him to. I don't want people knowing my business. When you think about it, his injuries, they're just little places in his back, are all your fault anyway. I told you that I didn't want an attorney, and since you made me take him, I should be able to treat him as I see fit."

"You're a nightmare." She smiled at the judge, knowing full well that he wasn't complimenting her at all. "David, I'm profoundly sorry this happened to you. Darrel, is he going to be all right?"

"Yes, sir. He will be, but I'd like to get him back to the hospital to have a few of these deeper ones looked at. Also, I want to make sure that there are no foreign objects, such as ink, in the wounds now that they're no longer bleeding." The doc, whoever he was, glared at her. "You're something else, aren't you? I hope you rot in prison."

"Well, aren't you a nice doctor? Like your opinion is going to sway the jury one way or the other." She winked at the cast of twelve, her favorite name for the idiots that were going to free her. "You guys don't bother thinking about this part of today. It's all water under the bridge now. I didn't hurt him all that much. He's just a pussy."

"You'll watch your language while in my courtroom." She mimicked the judge when he spoke to her. "Mr. Archer, I'm going to be adding assault to her attorney to the list of things that you're here for. Also, I'm going to fine her. And so that no one else is hurt by her, I'm going to allow her to represent herself. May god have mercy on her soul. If she even has one."

For the rest of the day, Susan objected to everything that the other attorney said to her and about her. It was the best fun she'd had in a long time. The judge was pissed off so much that he called lunch at ten, and when they returned, she started right back up on making sure that they didn't use shit against her that wasn't fair. Nothing had worked, of course, but she didn't let them off easy by telling people of the shit that they'd found out about her and Drew the day that she'd killed him.

At the end of the day, five-thirty had come too fast for her. The other guy said that he had presented everything that he had. When she was asked if she had anything to say to the jury, she decided that she did and stood up again. She asked if she could walk around as the other guy did, but she was denied that right and gave the man her worst glare when it was obvious to her that they were playing favorites.

Looking at the jury, dumb people, she thought,

Susan looked each and every one of them in the eye until they looked away first. It wasn't too long until she had every one of them fuckers looking in their lap. They were now going to do just what she wanted them to do or else.

"I didn't kill Drew, and you'd better be remembering that too. Because I will find out where you live. You can bet your life on that, and I do mean your life." No one moved in the jury box, and she felt satisfied that they'd do just what she told them to do. "I have nothing further to say."

"Did you...I'm not even going to ask that. You just threatened the jury with harm if they didn't tell me that you're not guilty." She said that she'd only told them the truth. "The truth is that you're going to hunt them down if they don't do as you threatened. I've had enough of you and your demands. But this, this right here is beyond...I'm going to sentence you myself. There is no reason whatsoever why you should be out where you can do more harm than good. You'll have my verdict in the morning."

"Is this the last night that I'm going to have to spend in that fucking cell?" He said that he'd make sure of it. "Good. I would hate to have to hunt you down as well. This has dragged on long enough."

He pounded his hammer or whatever it was on the desk and stood up. Before anyone could stand up like was required of them — another stupid thing that she was sick of — he was going through the little door at the side of the room.

Getting chained up this time wasn't so bad. Just knowing that she was going to be having a different place after this was making her in a good mood. It worried her a bit that he'd been so readily willing to get her out of the jail cell, but she had an idea that he was afraid of her. As well, he should be. She didn't get to where she was by fucking around with people who did her wrong.

The ride back to the jail was done in silence. Not that she had anything in common to talk to these people about, but it was nice to have a few minutes of quiet time to plan. And even though she didn't have anything to write with, she had a long list of things that she wanted to get done as soon as she was out. And she would be, too. Tomorrow was going to be a red-letter day, whatever that meant to her and the townspeople. Especially her family. They had fucked her over long enough.

~*~

Darrel had a plan to stay at his apartment that

night with Caitlyn. She seemed all right with the arrangements, and he didn't have to figure out a way to make sure that she was safe. It worried him to no end that Susan had been so vocal about threatening the jury and judge that he wondered what would happen with the judge. He'd dismissed the jury once he came back into the courtroom when Susan had been taken away. Holdom told them how very sorry he was that they'd been threatened. Darrel had been asked to stay when he had returned from taking care of David, and David was all right.

"Tomorrow morning, I'm going to set her sentencing without you being present. I'm sorry that you've been here for as long as you have. Once she is brought in tomorrow, you will be as safe as you could ever have been. This I promise you." One of the jurors raised their hand and asked a question. "No. You will not be required to give me a verdict on the case. I believe that, and I know that I'm right that you will not be held responsible in her eyes once you aren't here. It's the best possible scenario for keeping all of you out of harm's way. Anything else?"

Judge Holdom answered several more questions, mostly about how they would be able to return to work with a permission slip and what happened to their payment for having to spend their time here for nothing. As soon as he finished up with them, he sent them home with the caution of not speaking to anyone about what they'd thought about the trial.

Once they were gone, Holdom invited him back to his chambers for a talk and Darrel had been happy to go. As soon as they were seated, Holdom pulled out a bottle of whiskey and poured them both a nice full glass of the beautifully colored liquid.

"The one thing that I want to speak to you about is that I've had a phone call while I was here earlier. Doc Wellington passed away last night. It's not common knowledge to anyone that he had been suffering from heart failure for the last few years, but it caught up with him, his wife told me when he'd been asked to do the autopsy on young Snow." Darrel said that he would be missed. "Yes, he will. And I'd like for you to take over his job. I know it's a lot to ask of you. You've only just met that young woman and all but it would be a feather in your hat and make your momma proud of you too. I know you all, her sons and I know that you all live for making her happy. She's a hell of a woman, your momma."

"She is. And I'll take the job." Holdom laughed,

and he joined him. "It's been something that I've been striving for since I took my first forensic class five years ago. It both fascinated me and got me to thinking. I would be honored to do that job." He thought of something. "I should maybe talk it over with Caitlyn first. She might have other plans, and I don't want to step on her toes about this job."

"You are a good man. And yes, that will be all right with me if you need to talk to her. I'd expect no less from you." Darrel thought about the job and felt like he needed to run home right now and talk to her about it. "No one will rush you into the job, Darrel. You've been covering the job nicely for the past year now, and so long as there isn't any trouble until you make a sound decision, I have no doubt that you'll do a fine job for us and the county."

"Thank you, sir. Coming from you, that means a great deal to me." They finished off their drinks, and Darrel, who never drank, sat there blissfully feeling good while the drink relaxed him. "My sisters-in-law, Merce and Elizabeth, are due to have their babies any day now. I have been asked to deliver them. It will be all right with the county if I do some doctoring on the side, won't it?"

"Of course, it will be just fine." He closed his

eyes for a moment and opened them, actually waking up when he heard laughter. "I've called your young lady here for you. I believe you're intoxicated, young man."

"I believe that I might well be. I haven't felt this good in a long time." He asked him if he needed anything. "Yes. Will you marry me? I mean, marry me to Caitlyn? I've been meaning to set things up for a while now, and I'd like to make sure that she's...I don't know why I want to get a rush on this. But I feel like I should let her marry me so that she doesn't change her mind."

"It just so happens that I can do that for you." Darrel must have fallen asleep again because when he woke again, not only was Caitlyn there with him, but she was having a good laugh with the judge. "There he is. I'm thinking that after I get you two to sign off on the marriage certificate, you should take him home and put him to bed. I've been trying to keep him awake, but I think that he's a great deal more exhausted than I first thought."

He was asked to sign his name to something, and when Caitlyn told him that it was all right, he did so without reading anything over. His brothers would have killed him if they found out, but he trusted Caitlyn's judgment over theirs right now. As soon as he got into his truck, he was out again. Christ, he was going to have to get him whatever they'd been drinking in there. It was the best sedative he'd ever used.

Waking when the sun was blinding him from the open curtain, Darrel nearly got out of bed to close them when Caitlyn came out of the bathroom. She smiled at him as she put her earrings into her pretty lobes.

"About time. What the hell was in that drink that knocked you out for so long?" He said he didn't know but didn't feel too bad right now. "I would imagine not. You've been asleep since six o'clock last night. It's nearly nine now. Are you going with me to the courthouse?"

"I am." He leapt out of bed and into the bathroom. "Can you get me something to wear out of my closet? I'll just have enough time to get there if we walk. Finding a parking spot this late will be impossible."

They were in the courthouse at nine forty-five. The judge had three other cases that he was seeing over first he'd told them last night; Caitlyn told him and that he'd have a verdict on Susan by ten. He didn't want to miss what was going on with her, and he knew that Caitlyn didn't want to either. But they were surprised when her mother was there.

"Mom? I didn't know you'd be here." She told Caitlyn that she wanted to make sure that Drew got some justice for himself. She hugged her mom tightly and was so glad to see her there. "I gave our attorney everything you gave me the other day. He said that it went well with all the other evidence that he'd gotten, and we should see her going to prison."

Darrel was afraid of the verdict if he was honest with himself. Nothing went as well as he hoped, and this one, he was banking a lot of hope on. While he shook hands with not just Caitlyn's cousin, Terrance. He was glad to see that her aunt and uncle were there as well.

Abby was going on about how much Lynne looked terrible now that she was out of the nursing home and that she really should have taken the time to have had herself done up. While Darrel had no idea what the hell that might have meant, Lynne simply told Abby to shut up and to leave her alone.

"I've been grieving the loss of my son and husband that your daughter is directly responsible for. Now, either keep your trap shut, or I'm going to make it so that no amount of doing yourself up will help you with." He nearly laughed when Terry, Abby's husband, laughed. "And you, you should have taken care that she wasn't out and about like your brother told you to do when she was a child. She's been a menace since she was a baby, and you both knew it."

When Lynne asked him to escort her into the courtroom, he put out his arm to do just that. He did the same for Caitlyn, and the three of them had walked into the courtroom together. Whatever happened after this, he was happy that Caitlyn and her mom were able to do this together. The last few days of being around Lynne, he couldn't have had a better time. Darrel was going to see if he could convince her to come and live with them when they found a house.

The courtroom was called to order, and he watched as the judge looked as if he was in a terrible mood. It couldn't have boded well for Susan if he was already in a rotten mood before Susan was brought in. As soon as she was seated and chained to the desk, Wellington spoke.

"Last night, I was called no less than four times about Ms. Snow's behavior in her cell. I do not appreciate my having my sleep interrupted." Susan told him that he should have let her go when he'd had her in here yesterday. "Yes, you said that. Several times, as a matter of fact, when you finally were able to get directly to me. I've never looked so forward to having a sentencing as I am with you. You are the worst kind of person that I've ever encountered, and I've been on this bench longer than you've been alive."

"Perhaps you should get out of this job. You're too old anyway. Now, get on with it. I see that my family is here, so I can go directly home with them when you get off your ass and give me what I want." Susan looked around with a confused look on her face. "Where is the cast of twelve? Don't tell me that we have to get a whole new jury now. Christ, I can't keep doing this if you keep changing the shit around."

"They were dismissed." The judge asked for Susan to pay attention. "I don't want you to miss anything that I have to say to you."

"You'd better be telling me that I'm going home if you know what's good for you. I told you and anyone who will listen that I've stuff to do today. I'm sick of waiting for you to do your job. Another reason that you should retire or whatever. You're much too slow in your thought process to be judging people." She looked in his direction, and he knew she was speaking to Caitlyn when she spoke. "You'd better get your affairs in order, Caitlyn. I'm coming for you next."

"It gives me great pleasure to hand over the sentencing of Susan Abigail Snow." He put on his glasses before speaking again and started reading the paper that he'd picked up off his desk. "As for the threatening of a sitting judge, I sentence you to fifty years behind bars. For the threatening of a twelve-person jury, I sentence you to ten years for each person that you threatened. That comes to a total of one hundred twenty years." She asked him about her getting to go home today. "I'm speaking now, so you keep your mouth closed, or so help me, I'll tape it shut. Now, where was I?" He continued before she could say another word. "For the murder of Andrew Snow, I sentence you to life in prison without a possibility of parole. Additionally, another seventy years for abuse to a corpse. I've decided that I'd like to see you suffer as much as you have made those around you suffer." Susan asked him what that meant. "It means that I have found you guilty of the crimes that are being levied against you. You're just very lucky that I'm not giving you the death penalty for all the terrible things that seem to follow you around. You will leave here and be taken directly to the state penitentiary."

"No, that's not right. You said that I was going home. You had better fix this, or so help me, I'll make sure you hurt badly every day for the rest of your very soon to be death." He told her what he'd said. "That's not fair. You said that…you said that I'd be going home today."

"What I said to you, Ms. Snow, is that you'd not be spending another night in the jail cell that you've been incarcerated in and spending all your time in. And that is true. You're going to the big house along with all the other murders there." Darrel watched the two of them. One of them chained to the table in front of her, the other sitting much higher on his chair than he'd looked before speaking. "Now, if there are no other questions from anyone except Susan Snow, then I'm going to—"

"You can't be serious. Just what is it going to take for you to not put me in prison?" Wellington told her that he couldn't think of a single thing that would reverse his decision. "Well, you'd better be coming up with something. I'm not going to prison. I've told you that I have things that I need to take care of all along. There isn't any way that I'm going to be able to spend all that time—you told me that I wasn't going to jail."

"And you're not. You're going to prison." She actually stomped her foot at the judge. "It does me good to know that I got one over you, Ms. Snow. And as for your transportation to—"

"I want you to fix it so that I have a fine to pay." Susan looked around the room. "Any one of these idiots here can pay it. You make it happen, and things will go smoothly for you. Mom? Do you have your credit card on you?"

"I do. I really do, but I'm not going to bail you out, Susan. I wanted to, but then I thought about all the times that you hurt me and threatened me, and I just don't want to. You scare me at times." She told her that she'd not hurt her if she did this. "Yes, I knew you'd say that, daughter, but what happens when the next thing you do comes up? And you know that it will. You're not a very nice person. And killing Drew was the final straw for us all."

"Dad?" Her dad simply shook his head. "Terrance? Come on, buddy. Remember all the good times we had together? You have to have money, don't you?"

"I have money, yes. But I'm not going to waste it on thinking that you'd be better off out of prison than in it. Besides, you killed my best friend when you murdered Drew. He was a good person, and you decided that he had something that you wanted. Well, I know this is an old cliche, but you've made your bed now you can sleep it in for all I care." She asked him why everyone hated her so much. "Because, as you've been told, you're not a nice person at all. You're a murderer, and I'm glad that your bad deeds have caught up with you."

"This isn't going to fly with me." The judge asked her if she was ready to go. "No, I'm not fucking ready to go. I want out of here. Don't you get it? Yeah, sure, I killed Drew. Damn, it all to fuck and back. I hid his body, too. But don't you think that I've paid enough? I had to live for four years on the lamb because I didn't want to go to prison. Just fucking let me out of here, and I'll try my very best to be a good person for the rest of my free time. Do it now, and I won't call in some favors and have you killed, you mother fucker."

"I'm finished here." Judge Wellington left them

in the courtroom just as the police began filing into the room with them. They were dressed in armored vests as well as helmets on their head made to protect them. He was glad to see that they were taking things seriously and that she'd not be able to get away from them. But he still worried.

Darrel stood up when the police unchained her to take Susan away. He no more trusted her being able to get away from them and harming someone than he did anything else that was going on today. But as soon as she was out of the courtroom, yelling at her family to come and get her out of this, Darrel sat down and held onto Caitlyn's hand.

"Are you all right?" He nodded and kissed the back of her hand. "I'm glad to know that. I was worried about you for a moment or two. Are you sure that you're all right?"

"Never better. However, I've decided that you're going to be the one to tell my family that we're married and that I was half out of my mind with alcohol last night when it happened." She smiled at him and told him that she was glad that they had. "I am as well. I couldn't be happier."

Chapter 7

Caitlyn wasn't surprised that she'd gotten several phone calls from Susan over the last few days. She didn't answer her calls, nor did she leave messages to have her stop calling her. It would be funny for her if she were honest with herself. Every time she called her and left a message, it was like adding a year onto her sentencing for her. Caitlyn could well imagine that she was getting angrier and angrier with each message she left. Not that she ever listened to them.

"Why do you have such an odd look on your face?" Caitlyn smiled at Merce when she asked. The other woman had been wiggling around in her chair since they arrived for lunch. She and Elizabeth looked like they were ready to pop the two of them. She told her what was funny. "I bet that will stop soon, too. They'll be so mad at her for making everyone around her miserable that they'll not allow her to call you again."

"And until then, I'm going to enjoy slashing her hopes of getting me to do something with her. I won't, not ever, but it's been very satisfying for me to do this one last thing for her." Elizabeth asked her what she was going to do now that the trial was over. "I've decided to work with Darrel. I'm going to answer his phone for him and do some filing. For a little while, anyway. The woman who was working for him retired last week, and he's been busy looking for a replacement. I'm looking forward to doing something again."

"I heard you guys were able to close on that house you wanted. I was surprised to learn that it was your grandparent's home. Congratulations on that. I know what it feels like to have your own place. And getting to put out your own things. Has your mom made a decision on if she's going to be living with you two or not?" Caitlyn told Elizabeth what her mom wanted to do. "She wants to live in an assisted living place? I don't think that I would have thought that of her doing. You guys can give her round-the-clock care if she needs it, right?"

"She doesn't want to burden us. I kind of figured

that she'd say that. Not that she wanted to live in a condo for assisted living but that she'd think that she is a burden. But whatever makes her happy is all right with me. Also, she said that she could get around better than most of the people there, but she could also close her door when she didn't want to engage with them. She said that living alone is something that she's never done. She went from living at home to living with Dad, then onto the nursing home. I think she'll be happy there." Elizabeth seemed to be having some pain. "Are you all right? You look a little pale right now."

"I'm fine. Really, I am. I just have this nagging backache that is driving me crazy all the time. Once I find me a good position, it stops hurting for a while, and I can relax." Concerned, Caitlyn started to keep an eye on her phone clock so that she could be sure she wasn't in labor. "What are your plans for her house? I went by there the other day, and I saw a for sale sign in front of it. I didn't realize that it was such a big house before."

"When I was a little girl, and we'd go to her house for parties and such, she'd have a room for Drew and I all lined up. Some of the rooms have connecting doors, but most don't. We'd stay up late at night having the best time. Sometimes my grandda would come in and read us stories and have hot cocoa in his thermos." She smiled at the memory and looked down at her phone when Merce started making that squirmy movement that Elizabeth was making. "Are you guys due at the same time? I don't know that I ever heard."

"No. I'm due today, but I don't believe I'm close. I've not done that nesting thing that I've heard so much about. Elizabeth isn't due for another two weeks. I'll just be happy to have this over with. I want to hold my baby so badly. I know that Del is about to have a nervous breakdown. He wants it over, too, I guess." When their salads were brought to them, she very quietly messaged Darrel. Telling him where she was and what was going on, he said that he was in the mall area and would just happen by. "Did you know that Katie had all these guys at home? I didn't until the other day. She told me that once her babies were ready to be born, they wasted not one moment before they were ready to come into the world."

"You think that might happen to you guys?" After the salads were cleared, Caitlyn messaged Darrel to hurry his happy ass up. If they answered her, she didn't get it as Elizabeth spotted Darrel.

After hugs from them all, he had a seat next to her. "I was just in the mall, and I saw you guys. I'm glad to see you guys getting out and about." He watched both women, and she did as well. "Elizabeth, are you all right?"

"Caitlyn just asked us both that. I feel good." She looked pained for a few seconds. "I was telling her that my back is killing me. I know that there is a lot of pressure in my back now with the baby there, but it's been keeping me from sleeping well at night." She moved again, and Darrel turned his attention to Merce, who was looking very pinched.

"Merce?" She looked at Darrel and her. "Merce, you're scaring me a little bit. Tell me what you—"

"I think I'm in labor." She grabbed her hand and squeaked as she tightened her grip on her hand. "I know you called Darrel, and I was going to make fun of you for it, but I have a feeling that you're right, Caitlyn. I'm hurting."

"All right. We've plenty of time. Elizabeth, are you in labor too?" Any idiot could see that she was by just looking at her. Not only was her face pinched up, but so was her body. "I'm calling an ambulance right now. Just keep breathing, ladies, and we'll have some babies soon."

Caitlyn ended up riding to the hospital with Merce, while Darrel went with Elizabeth. Her contractions were harder, so Darrel didn't want to take the chance of her having the baby alone. As soon as they pulled up in front of the emergency room, she knew that something had happened. Darrel met them at the back of the ambulance.

"Elizabeth is seven cm and ready to go. I'm going to check you right here, Merce, to see who of you is going to go first. I'm betting on you. I haven't any idea why, but that's just me." He did the exam right there in the ambulance and laughed. "Yes. You're ready. Let's get this baby out into your arms, love."

Before they could get Merce out of the ambulance, she was crying out in pain. It took her one really good push against Darrel's instructions for her to deliver her little boy. She was still crying over Del not being there when they all heard Darrel's name over the intercom throughout the hospital. Staying with Merce and the new baby, Darrel ran into the hospital while Merce called Del.

Getting to hold onto the little boy, she couldn't believe how quickly he had come. While Merce was being cleaned up, still in the ambulance, she spoke to Del, Telling him not only did his son have all his fingers and toes, but he had his mother's hair and that he was about as handsome as she'd ever seen a little baby be. Then she turned the camera around so that he could meet his child.

Finding Darrel wasn't as hard as she thought it might have been upstairs. Following the sounds of a screaming newborn, she was thrilled when she found not just her little boy had been born, but he was being held by his daddy, Robert.

"Where are they?" She laughed when Katie came into the little room. "Oh my, I can't believe it. He's here."

Katie was holding the new baby when Darrel joined her in the room. He had on scrubs now and was in a great mood, she thought. Then he told his mom the great news that Merce had had her son, too, and that Del was on his way up to see them. He also told Elizabeth that he was going to have her transferred to the labor and delivery floor as soon as he checked her out.

"Same room." Darrel told her that they didn't have sharable rooms any longer. "Can you make it happen, Darrel? Please. We've been through this whole thing together so far, and I want to be with her now that we've had our babies. Please?"

"I'll see what I can do for you guys. But you both have to agree with it." Elizabeth said that she'd agree that they'd already talked about it. "All right. I'll work it out for the two of you. It will make it easier on me to check on the two of you while here."

"When can we get home?" Katie had left them then, going to see her other grandchild. "I want to take a shower in the worst sort of way."

"You should stay for at least twenty-four hours. For the babies. After that, if things are going well, I see no reason for the two of you not to be able to go home then. However, I'm going to only do this if you do what I tell you. Both of you need to rest as much as you can. No fucking around. All right?" She asked him if he thought that Robert was going to allow her to do anything when she was home. "I had hoped that he'd be here when I said that."

"She'll rest. I'll make sure of it." Robert hugged Darrel tightly and thanked him for making sure that his family was safe. "I love you so much, Darrel. I don't tell you guys that enough but I'm going to make sure that you know it daily, no, hourly from now on."

"Don't get mushy on me." They both laughed

and hugged again. "I love you too, Robert. Now, let me do my job and get your new family into a nice room so that they can rest up."

It was another couple of hours before the room was set up. They'd gotten bigger beds, the two of them, so that their husbands could lie down with them. The room was cramped, but they were happy, and Caitlyn thought that would make the healing process a good deal faster. Both couples were asleep before she and Darrel left the room to go home.

Since she'd missed her dinner, most of it anyway, Darrel fixed them a quick breakfast before she was out of the shower. Joining him in the kitchen just as the sun was coming up, Caitlyn thought that she was almost too tired to eat. But with Darrel talking to her, she did manage to get down most of it before she was nearly asleep on her feet.

"Tomorrow, I'm going to have to do rounds at the hospital. And I have three appointments in the morning at the clinic. What do you have planned for tomorrow?" She told him. "Good. I know that you'll get the filing system down easy enough. If you have any trouble, you can give her a call, right?"

"I can. I'm not worried about it overwhelming me." She wanted to ask him a question but didn't want to upset him with it. "We never talked about children. Did you want any?"

"I didn't. Not before you came along. I thought, like I did a wife, that it would be too burdensome for me. I haven't any idea why I thought that having a baby around wouldn't mean there would be a mom, too, but I had it in my head that I'd have to take on all the work when one was born to me." He smiled at her. "I do want children with you. As many as you'll give me. And I'm profoundly happy, more so daily, that you saw what a shithead I was and stuck with me. I don't know where I'd be if not for you in my life. It's almost as if I have been waiting for the right person to come along and save me from myself."

"I love you too, you big dork." After giving him a kiss goodbye, Caitlyn made her way over to the offices that Darrel was keeping. He was going to advertise for new patients, he'd told her, but not right now. They were planning not just to fix up their home but their honeymoon, too. She was going to see the world with him.

On her way over to the offices, she talked to a lot of people out and about. The weather had turned warmer today, but they were calling for snow tomorrow. It looked to her like everyone was out stocking up on supplies in the event the snow really did come through like they were predicting. Caitlyn didn't care. Wherever she wanted to go in town was within walking distance from the house.

Having the filing system already started and set up meant that she could easily jump right in and make sure that things were put away the way that they should be. Pulling out a couple of the files of the deceased patients, she was saddened to see that so many had passed away in the last year. The notes too that Darrel put on each one made her think that he was very close to all his patients. He was a good man. A very wonderful doctor, too.

Just as she was ready to leave, time had gotten away from her, and her cell phone rang. It was her mom. Talking to her while she locked up the office, she was happy that her mom seemed to be enjoying her time at the living center. If anyone deserved it, it should have been her mom. After making arrangements to have lunch with her at her place next week, Caitlyn made her way home.

It was a wonderful evening, and she stopped by the store to pick up some pork chops for dinner. They had fresh bread, too, just out of the oven, and she picked up a loaf of that as well. Getting to the cash register, she realized that she should have gotten a cart as her hands were too full to answer her cell.

"I just got a call from the prison. I wanted you to hear it before it was out on the news. Susan has gathered up hostages, they think about a dozen of them, and is at this moment carrying three guns. She's killed four officers as well as the Warden when he went to see her. Apparently, Susan asked to see him, and he went there. She didn't say a word, I was told, but shot him point blank in the head. She more than likely will be killed before this is over." She asked him how many were dead. "So far as they can see where she's holed up, eight. This isn't going to end well for her, honey."

"I know. She'll be killed shouting out to anyone who will listen to her that it's either all my fault or someone else's. Christ, she's a nightmare. What are we to do?" He told her what he'd been told. "Her parents aren't going up there, are they? And I know that Terrance has washed his hands of her, too."

"She wants you to come up as well so that she can do to you what she did to Drew." She asked him to repeat himself. "She's demanding that you come to the prison so that she can kill you. I'm not sure you should do that. I mean, no, she's not going to kill you, but to go up there now would be dangerous to you."

"What do you suggest?" He said that he was working on that. "All right. You work on a plan, and I'm going to call my uncle. Then Terance while I'm at it. If they go up there, then I will as well. I wouldn't be able to stand knowing that they're up there without me knowing what's going on."

After telling him where she was, he said that he'd pick her up. Caitlyn didn't know what was going to happen, but one thing she was sure of, Susan wasn't going to do this shit again to her and her family.

~*~

Darrel was able to help with the people that Susan had killed. They had a place set up where he could perform autopsies in and a freezer to store them in until arrangements could be made to bury them. Susan had managed to kill three more people as they made their way to the prison, and she was running out of time, the acting warden had told her.

Susan kept screaming at Caitlyn to be brought to her. Also, her brother. She wouldn't speak to her parents after they begged her to give up this stance she was taking. Firing at them when they wouldn't leave when she told them to, Susan had managed to injure her father in the leg with a bullet. Abby was in hysterics, but Caitlyn told him this was normal for her. That no matter what he did for her, she'd be just as crazy. Darrel thought that the entire family was crazy on that side of the family.

After planning and planning, he still wasn't thrilled about what they had planned for Susan, but it was better than her killing off her hostages one at a time. When Caitlyn was dressed in heavy armor with a helmet over all of her head, she went to stand down the hall from the cell she was in. He was happy for the camera that Caitlyn was wearing so that everyone could see what Susan was up to. He'd be more happy if the camera was on someone else but they were getting desperate.

"Why are you dressed like that, you moron? How am I to make you pay for me being here?" Caitlyn told her that she didn't care. "You will care if I have to fill you full of holes to kill you. Take it off."

"No. And if you demand only that I take off this gear instead of telling me what you're doing, then I'm going back home. You're going to end up on the wrong end of a bullet with this, and I find that I don't give a fuck about it. What is it you want?" Caitlyn laughed. "I'm not going to give you anything or do anything for you, but I will ask you. What?"

"You weren't answering my phone calls." Caitlyn asked her if that was all. "No, it's not all. Fucking bitch. You should be getting me out of here instead of ignoring me all the time. This is all your fault. Why did you have to keep searching for your brother when I didn't want you to."

"I believe you know the answer to that. He was my brother, and I wanted to know who killed him. No, that's not right. I knew you'd done it, but I wanted my mom to have peace with the fact that he was really gone." Caitlyn moved around one of the bodies that were outside the cell. Even going so far as to pick up his badge so that the people he was with could see his name. "Why did Will have to die? There was no reason for you to have murdered him."

"Yes, there was. He was in my way. And I don't know why you've not come to realize this or not, but when people are in my way, they tend not to live long. I want you dead, Caitlyn. I have hated you since you were born." Caitlyn asked her what she'd done to her as an infant. "They gushed over you. My parents said you were the prettiest baby they'd ever seen. I was standing right there when they said that to your parents."

"So? You've turned into a beauty. More beautiful…well, you used to be beautiful. Since you've been a mad person all your life, you've turned out to be very ugly. Why are you like this, Susan? No one I know is like this? Not on either side of our family." The shot to the armor must have knocked Caitlyn down, but she told them as she got up that she was fine. "So you're going to waste your bullets on firing at me when you know there isn't any way that you can kill me. You're not only ugly, Susan, but you're also stupid. Just think about where you are and what you've done here. Do you think that they're going to let you go? That anyone is going to trust you ever again? Christ, you've killed so many people now that you'll be lucky that you don't get the chair for this. Do we even have that in Ohio?"

"While they haven't had one occur in the last five years, it's still in place." Darrel was happy for the earbuds that he and Caitlyn shared. He was also happy that she told him that she wasn't hurt by the shot to her belly. "Good to know. Also, when you get out of here, I'm going to fuck you hard, babe."

"Good. I will need it. After a long, hot shower. I feel nasty, right—"

"Who the fuck are you talking to — you have a communicator on? You're talking to others instead of paying attention to me?" She was shot three more times, but all it looked like was that it made her stagger back. Again, she said that while painful a little, it wasn't as bad as it could have been. "Who is that you're talking to?"

"My husband." Susan told Caitlyn that she wasn't married. "Oh, but I am. To a doctor, no less. And he loves me to pieces. Also, and this just occurred to me, I'm never going to tell my children about you other than the fact that you murdered their uncle. You're not going to have a name for them. Just this person who was insane and killed not just their grandfather, my dad, but my brother as well."

"Good girl. You keep that up. The man that is going to shoot Susan is about to enter the hallway where you are. Remember, honey, don't get in front of her. I don't know what I'd do if you were hurt." She told him that she loved him. Then she told him that she could see the sharpshooter now. "Keep her distracted, and this will be over soon."

"You're going to do what I tell you, Caitlyn, or so help me. I'm going to kill these people here. I've had enough of your dicking around with me." When

Susan raised her gun up and pointed at Caitlyn, Susan dropped out of sight.

Darrel heard the all clear and made his way to his wife. But he couldn't touch her just yet. She was still in the armor, and there was blood all over her. The head wound to Susan ended her life and saved the lives of the other nine people who were with her.

"I'm all right." He nodded, unable to make a sound when her helmet was removed, and he could see her lovely face. "I hurt a little from the impact, but they told me that would happen. I am truly all right, Darrel."

"I believe you. But I still want to make sure." She nodded and turned to look where Susan was lying in her blood. "Cait, honey, look at me, not her. It's done and you don't need to be dwelling on what might have been with her. She's gone. And you and the rest of us are safe."

Once he was given the all-clear to touch her, he pulled her into his arms and held her tightly. He knew in his mind that she was all right, but it still terrified him in ways he'd never felt before that it could have gone so wrong, too.

"I love you." He told her that he loved her too. So much. "I want to have children now, Darrel. I want to have a little one in my arms that you and I created out of love and happiness. Then I want to never think about this day and the days leading up to it again about Susan. It's done. All right?"

"Yes. I agree with you on all accounts. A child growing in you is the best thing I think a person could want. I love you so much, Caitlyn. With all that I am."

They were asked to fill out some paperwork about what had happened. Darrel was more than happy to be the one who signed the death certificate on Susan. While he was doing that, Caitlyn called her aunt and uncle to tell them what had happened. From what he could hear on Caitlyn's end, it was a relief to both of them. Terrance, who had come to the prison with them, held onto Caitlyn as she explained to him what had happened.

He'd been there, of course. Terrance had come up with them, but he let Caitlyn tell him. It was cleansing for them both, Darrel thought. To be able to say that it was over and that Susan wouldn't harm them any longer.

Going home, he was glad for the limo to take them there. Neither of them was in any kind of shape to drive safely, and Caitlyn seemed to need the extra love that he was able to give her. He knew that, on some level, she was feeling guilty about what had happened. He supposed that he would as well. But it was over, and even though it might take them some time to get over it, he felt good about the fact that Susan was gone for good.

"There won't be a funeral for her. Any kind of services for her, as a matter of fact. Uncle Terry is going to let them bury her on the prison grounds. He doesn't want a place where Aunt Abby can go and visit her. He's afraid that she'll switch things around in her mind, and that won't do her a bit of good." Darrel said that he had heard that as well. "I don't know that it will make her any less good that her daughter is gone as to where she is buried, but that's what he thinks. I'll be there for him if he needs me. Will you?"

"Of course. I'll do whatever he needs me to do. For both of them." She thanked him, and he had to smile. "You're worrying too much about things. I want you to just relax for a little while."

"I'm fine." He knew that while she kept saying that, he had a feeling that she was far from it. Seeing someone shot and to have it done to a relative, too, was something that was going to haunt her for a long while. He only hoped that she would be all right in the end so that it didn't bother her forever. "I'm suddenly exhausted. I want to go home and soak in a tub for an hour and melt into the bed."

"I can help you with that. Once you're relaxed enough that I have to scoop you out of the tub, then I'm tucking you into our bed and letting you rest while I watch over you." She nodded, and he felt her body relax little by little. He was sure that she was asleep by the time they were pulling into the driveway of their home.

Chapter 8

It was midnight when his phone rang. Sitting up in bed, Darrel answered with a question. "Is it time?" Darrel's son, Adam, laughed and told him that it was time and that they were on their way to the hospital right now. And would he like to join them?

Darrel didn't have to wake Caitlyn to tell her what was going on. As soon as the phone rang, she hopped out of bed and ran to the bathroom. Telling Adam that they were on their way had his youngest son laughing.

"Dad, you do know that it's going to take a while." Adam laughed again. "Carrie didn't want me to call you this soon as she said that you'd come right away no matter how long it took. But she knew that you'd be upset with us, and she didn't want that. Not today, anyway. Dad, I'm going to be a dad soon."

"That you are. I'm so proud of you. And I knew that I loved that girl more than you. Yes, we'll wait to the ends of the earth for this to happen." Hanging up the phone, he got up and did a little jig around the bedroom. Another grandbaby coming into the world. Getting dressed was easy. He'd had his clothing laid out for weeks, waiting for his grandbaby to be born.

It wasn't like this was their first grandchild. All his sons had married now and were well on their way to populating the world with little Archers. He had to take a deep breath when he thought of how much his mom had missed since she'd passed on. It was then that he realized that it was her birthday today. How wonderfully fitting, he thought. And more so, what his grandda had missed as well.

They both had died on the same day. Mom had gotten cancer and had died on the morning of December twelfth, fifteen years ago. And grandda had gone to bed that night, broken-hearted and passed too. He told them all that he just couldn't lose any more people in his life and that their mom had been as close to a daughter as he'd ever had. He had always known that they were close as blood relatives, and having grandda living with Mom had done them both a world of good.

Their funerals had been private, but that didn't stop hundreds of people from coming by to offer them their condolences. For days after the funeral, people would drop by one or all of their homes to tell a story about one or both of them. Darrel missed them so much that it hurt him to his core when he realized once again that they were gone.

The drive to the hospital was short but seemed much longer because they were both so excited. When they were headed up to labor and delivery, he held Caitlyn's hand. He couldn't love her any more than he did right then. She had given him the greatest gift in loving him. Then, when their sons came along, it was as if he loved her more than before. She was his everything, and he didn't know what he'd do without her.

They, just as he predicted, didn't have long to wait. Adam's brother, Lance, came to be there with them, bringing his children along with him and his wife. He was holding the youngest grandchild before this one, Sara Jane, in his arms when Adam came out to tell them that the baby had been born and that she was as beautiful as her mom was.

Darrel kissed Caitlyn and held her as she sobbed

over the news. This was their fifth grandchild and their third granddaughter. It was nice, he thought, having all the little girls around after having five sons of their own. He especially loved the holidays with them all. Little girls were the best, he thought. Then, he remembered how much fun he had with the boys when they came over to play on the swing set that they'd put in the year that their oldest son, James, had gotten married.

"Grandpa D, can I sit in your lap, please? I find that I'm a little nervous for this new baby." He handed the baby off to her grandma and pulled Joey up into his lap. This little one at six had the most to say about things. He reminded him daily of his dad, Lawrence, his second oldest. Joey would find him when he needed some cuddling. However, he never called it that anymore. Joey was too big for cuddles, he'd told him once. "You know what I was thinking about? I don't think that I want to have a wife with babies. It makes everyone kind of weird, don't you think? Especially when there are little babies around. Women especially get all ga-ga when they see them. Don't you think?"

"It does, I guess. But it's a good kind of weird. I mean, look at all the happiness in this room.

Remember what Grandma said about happiness and how it makes the ill feel better? I believe that all the time." Joey laid his head on his chest and watched the people in the room with them. "You have a lot to teach this little one, don't you think? I mean, who is going to teach her how to jump rope and swing up as high as you can? Or how to bait a hook when you take her fishing. She's going to need your expertise in a lot of things. It'll have to be you, my man. I'm getting too old to swing much anymore."

Joey turned and looked at him. Darrel let him look all he wanted without speaking. Joey was the thinker of the grandchildren, and once he spoke, you knew that whatever he had to say was going to be profound, for as much as a six-year-old could be considered profound.

"How old are you, Grandpa D?" He told him that he was nearly eighty-eight. "That's really old, huh? I mean, you're not as old as my uncles, but you're getting up there."

"Yes. It's really old. But I can still tickle you until you scream." He didn't laugh as he hoped he would. "What is it, son? What are you thinking about? You know that you can tell me anything that you have on your mind. And that I'll be there for you when you and I both have to find the answers. What is it, buddy?"

"I was just thinking about something. I guess that someday you're going to die, too, huh? It hurts me something terrible when I think about that." He nodded. The emotional turmoil going through his mind right then kept him from speaking. "I don't want you to leave me, Grandpa D. I know that you won't promise me that you won't die, but you have to take care of yourself so that I can learn all I can from you. All right? You're my best friend in the whole wide world and I don't know that I could learn anything from anyone else. You're very special to me."

"Yes, I'd like that too. And you're very special to me, too, Joey. You always have been." Hugging Joey, they sat there for several more minutes while the others around them were talking. Darrel had to wipe his tears away several times as he thought about what his grandson had said to him.

Darrel held Joey until he began to squirm around on his lap. Taking him to the bathroom when he said he had to go, Darrel decided that he was going to spend more time with the grandkids and his own kids as much as he could. He didn't know how much time he had left in this old world, but he was going to make every moment of it a memory that he could take with him into the afterlife. Hopefully, that was a long way away, and that he could really teach them all the things that he knew before pushing up daisies.

After the two of them washed up, they headed to the nursery. Just the two of them watched as baby after baby were fed their bottles and put back in the cribs. It was a memory for him that jumped into his mind and made him think of the day that he'd delivered Merce's and Elizabeth's babies. Smiling, he told Joey about it.

"You should have seen them. Acting like they weren't ready to have their little ones. If not for your Grandma C, I think they would have sat there until they had the babies in the restaurant." Joey looked up at him, smiling, telling some of the story as he'd heard it a million times, he'd bet. "Yes, that's right. Grandma C messaged me to tell me everything that was going on."

He'd been telling stories to his grandchildren since they'd been infants. Not just about things that he'd done but things that he remembered about his grandda and mom. There were plenty of pictures, too, that he would tell them about. Mom had been big on taking pictures and having them developed. He would continue on to tell them things about their great-grandmother and their great-great grandda. The good with the bad, too. Not that there was too much in the way of bad stories about their other grandparents, but he didn't mince words about how much he loved them either.

When his brothers showed up with their wives, it was quite crowded in the room. But it was all right, he supposed. They were giving out hugs, and he was all for it. It occurred to him, standing there waiting for his turn to get hugs, that they were all looking very old of late, including himself, if a six-year-old noticed it. It saddened him terribly when he thought of losing another one of them someday. Hugging Peter when it was his turn, Darrel hugged him just a little tighter than he might well have earlier.

Peter, the oldest, was in his wheelchair now, and since his wife Heather had passed on. Peter had been living with his oldest son since her passing. He didn't like living with his son. Darrel knew that. He felt like a burden to them. Darrel might well, too, if he had to move in with one of his children. But he seemed to be in good spirits today, so that made him think that things were going well for him. Peter had plenty of stories to tell about their growing up together with their parents and he enjoyed them as much as the kids did.

He missed Heather a great deal. Darrel would often just hang out with his brother and her just to have someone to argue with. And she was good at it, too. Even if you could prove her wrong, she didn't back down. He thought that she enjoyed it too when he would come to their home and missed that more than anything. She forever had something baking in the oven that they'd share. She couldn't cook, not worth a damn, but she could bake anything and everything she found a recipe for.

William was getting around well, he noticed. He, too, had lost his wife, Tally, but she'd been in a car accident that had taken not just her life but one of their grandchildren as well. It had devastated them all when they found out. The baby, a little girl, had only been six months old when she died of complications of the accident. Tally had died a few days later from the same thing, but he had a feeling that she felt bad for the baby being with her, and that had just about broken her heart. He knew that it would his if that had of happened to him.

Someone had run a stop sign and hit them, going about sixty miles an hour. Tally had been injured so badly in the accident that there had been not even a way for her to donate her organs. Her death had put William in a deep hole for a long time that none of them thought that he'd come out of. But once his children came to see him more often, William not only came out of the deep depression that he was in, but he seemed to take on a better outlook on life.

Darrel had taken a few notes from his brother, too, in living each day to the limit. He was glad to see that William was excited to see the newest member of the family. He did mention that Tally was going to brain him for not being the first to hold the baby. He said that same thing when his own grandkids had been born. Just to see if anyone fell for it and let him hold the baby first.

Darrel didn't know what he'd do if something happened to his Caitlyn. Like his brothers, he thought he might just lay down and die with her. He loved her so much that he couldn't imagine life without her. He didn't want to. That was when he thought about what he'd said to Joey about staying around, and his heart hurt a little. He loved that little boy more than anyone, he thought, and wasn't ashamed to admit it.

Robert and Elizabeth were the last to show up. But they had food for them all, so it was easy to forgive them. Robert had had a stroke a few years ago. It had him too looking into a new outlook on life. He had to use a cane now, but he didn't seem to mind. It was refreshing for him to see his brother still hugging his wife and holding Elizabeth's hand when they were together. They were the cutest couple, he thought. Still, to this day, he loved watching the two of them being together.

Elizabeth still volunteered at the homeless shelter one day a week, giving medical help to those who needed it. There were quite a few that still needed a little help around, and he would help out when he could. Robert had encouraged her to get out of the house and away from him after he'd had his stroke for a little while. Being a doctor, too, she fussed too much over his brother, and rather than fighting about it, he told her to go to the shelter. Even Robert would go there when he could get around, and people were happy to see them both.

Sherman and Marcia were both gone now. Sherman had had a heart attack when he'd been in his fifties and never really recovered from it. He missed his brother and Marcia. They were the first of them to go, and it bothered him endlessly that he couldn't go and talk to him when he wanted. However, he did make his way to the cemetery once or twice a month. Just to clean off the weeds from around his marker and to tell him what he'd been up to. Not much, he supposed, but it was nice to do this for himself.

Marcia had been a good wife to him while he was trying to recover. But her own heart had been too weak to live through her own heart attack just before Sherman had passed away. Sherman had gone to a nursing home instead of living with his oldest daughter after Marcia had passed. She wanted him there. Little Marcia, their daughter, what they all called her, had begged for him to come and stay with them. But he had been determined. Sherman hadn't even made it a whole day without getting to set foot into the nursing home before he'd had another heart attack that took him from them. He died at home, in the same bed that he'd shared with Marcia his entire married life. His heart had just been too weak to live without his love, Darrel knew.

He thought that they'd made a pact, the two of them, that they'd not live without the other. Like his mom and grandda, the two of them passed away within hours of each other, and they were laid to rest through all of eternity together as well. He and Sherman had been the closest of all his family. And it hurt him as freshly as if he had only just died today whenever he thought of having one less brother to go to when he needed it. He wanted to go to the grave now and talk to him, to tell him of the new baby. But he'd wait at least until tomorrow to go tell him.

Del, being the youngest of all of them, was getting around better than any of them were. He'd been taking care of himself since he'd been a teenager. He'd been the only one who had played sports and he thought that he'd gotten staying healthy from his days playing ball. Whatever it was, he looked like a man half his age. He still worked at his job with his boys. Merce had passed her part of the business that she and Del had formed long ago down to her oldest son.

Delmar was doing a great job making sure that it was a good company that ran well and was fair to their employees. It had grown, too. The company was all over the world now, making things for hospitals and other places to make things easier in places. Especially hospitals.

When he got the opportunity to hug Del, he was surprised to have him hug him so tightly. Looking at his younger brother, he asked him what was wrong. Shaking his head, Darrel asked him again. His brother asked him if he knew what today was.

"Yes, it's mom's birthday." Del nodded and blew his nose into a tissue he'd had. "Are you all right?"

"Yes. Just thinking about how much she's missed. I mean, she was here for a lot of the grandkids, but I miss talking to her. Do you?" Darrel nodded again, overcome with so much emotion that it closed off his throat. "As we were getting ready to come in here to be with you, all I could think about was that she'd be in her element about now. All these little ones coming around and with her."

"I was thinking of grandda too. Wouldn't he have been acting like he invented grandchildren? I can almost imagine what he'd be saying about now." They both laughed. "Mom would be knitting up so many booties and blankets for them all that we'd have to buy yarn in bulk for her."

"Yeah, that's right. Do you remember where she put all those little booties that she made when she was younger? I swear to you, I think she knew that we'd have all these kids around for her to love. I'm going to have to find out where they are." He told him that he thought that Peter had them. "I think you might be right on that. I'm going to talk to him when we get out of here. Have you seen your newest yet?"

"Yes. He thankfully looks like his mother." They laughed again, the two of them. And that brought the rest of them to come to find out what they were laughing about. "We were talking about it being Mom's birthday. And how much she'd love all this."

"She'd be out of her mind with happiness." Once they started talking about their mom, the five of them couldn't stop bringing up stories that he was sure had been told a million times by them. Even the grandkids knew the stories and would tell parts of it with them.

~*~

Joey watched his grandda breathing. His mind was telling him that his breathing was much better, but his heart was telling him that his breaths were coming slower and slower. Grandda was an old man with an old heart, and it was worn out, he'd told him earlier in the day. He didn't want his grandda to pass. He and him had had a wonderful life, and he wasn't ready for it to end. Not ever.

"I love you, grandda. I can't thank you enough

for keeping your promise to me and sticking around for me until I learned all I could from you." His grandda was nearly ninety-nine years old now, and he was exhausted. "I'm also glad that you stayed long enough for me to love you more than anyone in the world."

At eighteen, Joey had been his happiest with his grandda. Once his grandma C had passed away four years ago, Joey had asked if he could live with his grandda, and he had been there since. Right now, doing the very thing that had been asked of him, he and his grandda were the only two people in the house, and his favorite person of all time was passing away right in front of his eyes, taking a huge piece of his heart with him.

"I did call my dad to let him know that the end was coming. But just like he said you'd do, you're hanging on to life when it's been too hard on you. Grandma C is waiting for you." He sobbed hard when he thought about his grandma passing in the same way, with only grandda and him there to be with her when she was gone. "She's fussing at you, and you know it. I can hear her now."

He and his grandda had made every single day an adventure. When the weather was too much for them to be out in, they would look up things to get them into trouble on the computer. Joey had seen the world with his grandparents, and he wouldn't have it any other way.

"I was thinking about the day that old dog came into the yard and started putting up a ruckus about how we were on the porch. I don't think he cared one bit that we were there because we owned the place, but he was just a mean old bastard." Joey looked around to see if his mom was nearby. Even though she told him that his age might make him an adult, he wasn't in her book. "You should rest easy in knowing that I've decided to take you up on the deal to live here with my own family someday. After I get out of college."

Joey knew his grandda's will had given him everything. He was to divide the money, and there was a great deal of it between all the grandkids. The house and the contents belonged to him. The two of them had spent a lot of nights going over the things that Joey would keep or not. It was going to be difficult, he knew, even though he had a list to part with anything that either of his grandparents had touched.

His breathing was slower now. There was no

denying it. He could almost count to five between breaths. His heart pained him so much then that he had to rub it to make sure that it was still beating in his own chest. The end was coming, and even though he had known this day would come, it still hurt him to know that tomorrow, he'd be alone without his grandda and grandma.

Grandda had lived the longest of all the Archer boys. Del, even being the youngest, had died much too soon for him. All he'd done was close his eyes one night and hadn't woke up. Grandda had told him that Del had had the biggest smile on his face when he'd seen him to make him think that he'd found the biggest secret. Whatever he'd been thinking about, Aunt Merce had smiled the same way when she told the story to the kids.

The others had died soon after that. One at a time, the Archer boys, as his great grandma had called them, went to be with their wives and mom. While he didn't personally know his great-grandma, there were stories that he could tell about her that would make one think that he grew up with her by his side.

"I did pick up your suit for you to wear. And the shirt that he wanted. I'm betting that Grandma C is going to give you what for when you show up there with that bright yellow shirt on. You'll have to tell me about it when I come to see you." Not for a long while, he thought the same words that his Grandpa would tell him when he'd ask for him to tell him when he got to heaven with him. "I know not to put anything in the paper until you're gone, but I'm sure that the entire town will know that you've passed. You had a way about you, grandda, that people just knew when you were around. I don't doubt that they'll have that same feeling when you're gone. Christ, I'm going to miss you so much, Grandda."

He cried softly for a little while. Joey had never been ashamed of shedding tears. Grandda and his own father had told him that tears were the way to wash out the soul. And a way to grieve when it was necessary.

Grandda had never made him feel like he was less than a person just because he was handicapped. Being born without his left hand had given him difficulties, but it never made him unable to do what he wanted. He owed that to his parents, then his grandparents. He didn't even remember most of the time that he had been born without it. That's how good and perfect that his family, all of them, had made him feel.

Joey realized that he'd fallen asleep when he woke up startled. Grandda's hand was laying on his shoulder then, but he was gone. Not knowing how long he'd been passed hurt him, but he knew that it was easier on the two of them for knowing that neither of them suffered overly much. Getting up after putting his hand back under the quilt, he made his way to the kitchen to make the calls that he had to make.

When his dad answered the phone, he didn't speak. He couldn't. Sobbing on the phone, his dad seemed to understand and told him that he'd be there soon. Nodding, not really caring if he could see him or not, Joey hung up the phone and called the police. It was the next name on his list of things to do.

For the next several hours, he fielded answers to the questions as they were put to him. After Dad and Mom showed up, he let them answer what they could. It seemed as if the entire town was there when he made his way to the living room. He had to smile a little, thinking that he'd been correct. The town would know when he passed away.

"Did he say anything to you, son?" Joey told his dad that he and grandda had had a nice conversation earlier in the day, but he'd been so tired that he went to bed. "He told you, didn't he, that he was ready."

"He did. He said that he'd been thinking a great deal about Grandma and knew it was time for him to go. He said to tell you that he loved you and all of the others, but he said that he was happy that you and the rest were allowing him to go out this way. I'm going to miss him so much." Dad held him while he cried out his sorrow again. "He stuck around for me, you know that, don't you? I asked him to stay with me, and he did."

"He told me that he couldn't promise you anything that day, but he was determined to do it for you." Nodding, he hugged his dad again. "You're a good son, Joey. Better than I would have thought about being my son, and you know that I expected no less than perfection from all my kids."

"Yes, I know." The laughter was just what he needed, and he was glad that his dad was there for him. "I'm going to go to college in the fall. He made me promise. He said that I was to have this first adventure on my own so that I could tell him about it someday."

"You do that. For both of you." When Grandda was removed from his bedroom and taken out to the ambulance, Joey found himself in the bedroom, sitting on the bed. He still had things to do, but all of it could wait until morning. Right now, he was about as exhausted as he'd ever been.

Lying on the bed, he pulled the quilt up and over him and took a deep breath. It still smelled like him, and he thought that he'd never wash it. Joey would need it someday, and he wanted it to be right here where they had had their last conversation.

"I'm going to miss you so much, you old buzzard, but I'm also going to be happy that you're not hurting anymore. You told me that getting old was for the young—not that I ever understood that, but I believe you." His body began to close down with the exhaustion, and he knew that he'd be asleep soon. His parents would make sure that things were taken care of for now. "You told me not to mourn you like that is going to happen, but I won't dwell on it too long. As you told me, I have a long life to live, and I'm going to get right on it. I love you, grandda, and I will see you on the other side one day with so many memories that you'll be sick of me talking to you."

AWARD WINNING, BESTSELLING AUTHOR

Kathi Barton, a winner of the Pinnacle Book Achievement Award and a best-selling author on Amazon and All Romance books, lives in Nashport, Ohio, with her husband, Paul. When not creating new worlds and romance, Kathi and her husband enjoy camping and going to auctions. She can also be seen at county fairs with her husband, an artist and potter.

Her muse, a cross between Jimmy Stewart and Hugh Jackman, brings her stories to life for her readers in a way that has them coming back time and again for more. Her favorite genre is paranormal romance, with a great deal of spice. You can visit Kathi online and drop her an email if you'd like. She loves hearing from her fans. aaronskiss@gmail.com.

Follow Kathi on her blog: http://kathisbartonauthor.blogspot.com/